MW00876206

Yang but Yin:
The Legend of Miss Dragonheel
by
Garrett Murphy

© 2013 Garrett Murphy
All Rights reserved.

ISBN-13: 978-1481947688
ISBN-10: 1481947680

to Faith Davis

Prologue

She wanted to stay prostrate on the cold night sidewalk and let the cold breeze or whatever else came by to just do what it would to her. Cast out by family, cast out by job, cast out by all...and now by her own yet again.

They had laughed uproariously and shoved each other with their pipe dreams of a Superior Nation and about starting applications for this nation as if such were ever possible. She had offered to be the first applicant.

"You? Apply for citizenship to OUR nation?"

"Lady get real. This here's for us only!"

Yet she was one of them.

"Shit go back to your whiteass suburb."

Oh those poor fools they had been. Fancying themselves superior when they couldn't even tell their own was one of theirs half the time. Of course that had made them mad when she told the truth to them.

"You better shut the fuck up here and now."

"SHUT UP BITCH!"

The old macho approach. Typical of an inferior per---

Same with the blows that had followed and coup de graced with the one that had sent her crashing to her current position on the sidewalk, half-conscious.

"Crazy whiteass cunt!"

"Imagine her fucking thinking she was fucking one of us," they had muttered as they walked away.

She was still one of them.

She wanted to stay prostrate on that cold night sidewalk and let whatever vulture came to take her away to where she could be free and happy and wanted at last. Oh please let me stay down and waste away, who would miss this pathetic drunken--
-

No you don't woman. C'mon you foolish Miss Dragonheel you've never let a setback beat you before don't you dare start now you've risen too many times to go down.

Her body ached, protested and wanted to stay but the mind was insistent, forcing her head to move so she was looking forward, in front of her. One stockinged foot groped its way along the sidewalk in search of something. Before long it found its objective, the stilettoed shoe that had come off when she had been dropped to the ground. With some fidgeting, the two were reunited.

The battle was on. First round to the body which impacted once more with the pavement. Second round---mind makes headway but body takes this one too.

Third round---mind goes all out in the titanic struggle against body's mass and gravity's pull. Forcing the feet to find traction, mind finally prevails, achieving the breakthrough and forcing body into an erect yet wobbly stance, leaning against a telephone pole for support and triumph.

See you did it! No little match girl you.

And besides, it's not even raining. And when was the last time it ever snowed in these parts!

One

From within the massive branches of the oak tree in her back yard, Florence could observe the rear of her Italianate Villa home and the well-kept if unspectacular yard several feet below her. At those times she occasionally imagined herself a leopard or panther looking upon all below her.

In childhood she could never have engaged in such ecstasy. *Get your pale tail down out of there I'll tan you till you're* really *colored don't you damage your dress don't you let your drawers show you want me to color your butt in with my switch you want your shoes to slip and make your pale ass fall and put a color on your hide* I'LL *put a color on your hide get your whiteass butt outta there YESTERDAY!!!* Well, she was free of that now, long free, of the job run out of her and even more of the jailers of her childhood, so she could be up there as long as she wanted, let her drawers show as much as she wanted (or hell, not even *have* drawers!) and damage her dress as she pleased. Let it get damaged, let the shoes, dragonheel spikes and all---slip. Even let herself fall! Couldn't be much worse than the falls she'd already suffered, especially after she'd been found out and the years of the career she had invested so much into become one huge waste and *friends* and *associates* had dropped off like rats fleeing a disabled ship Fall indeed---who was left to care? Certainly not that damned fool Dashiki Drab! And not her---there were adventures to be had in her---*her*---huge oak tree---a smorgasbord of overhead caves and paths and passages. She wanted the gropes, the caresses,

7

the embrace of her flesh against its solid wood. She even wanted the slides, the slips, the occasional difficulty with toeholds and footing. Small prices for the satisfaction of explorations long denied her----the fictional treasures of unknown lands, the rescues of men or boys in distress, the views of varying types of lairs and the quests for scrolls of knowledge or wisdom from some malleable sage. The brothers had their fun; now it finally was her turn.

On occasion there were a few near falls, and on rare occasions she actually did lose her hold and fall to earth, usually on her back or side but once on her face, but (given her age and attire) surprisingly seldom, and her worst injury had been a split lip (from when she landed on her face). But usually (and more often than not on Florence's whim), only a shoe, sometimes both---drop off her foot or feet and made the way to the ground as a sacrifice for appeasing some woman-eating predator or in exchange for some knowledge or clue to her objective. Allowing her legs and feet (or one of each) to dangle loosely overhead, she would relax, ease and flex her foot until the shoe slid off and made its sweet descent. And the quest would go on until completion.

Another amusement for her was the fantasy of dropping a shoe on some bullying elder (*Get your light ass down that UMMMMPHHHHH!!!!!* "Not anymore, *mom-mie*," she smirked. "*My* place now.") Or that bum Dashiki Drab who was always berating her (*You mind your elders you know your plAAAAAAAAAAKKKKKKKK!!!!!*) *Silly Garveyites.* And afterwards, Florence made her way down to the soft grass with an ease one would consider surprising for one her age and dressed as she was, dress and stockings well worse for wear, but no matter---she casually retrieved her shoe or shoes and moved in triumph to the womb of her Italianate Villa, content with the release of herself and her energies.

Two

The headlines of her fall remained fresh in her mind even a bit over a year later, she knew as she viewed a videotape compilation of the fall of Miss Dragonheel herself, a Ms. Florence Orville (dubbed the above nickname after a co-worker's wry remark about her determined temperament and footwear). She was too obsessed with her own ordeal, was aware others would have insisted on her *getting over it!* Sure. Easy to insist when you're not the one who's taken the fall.

The pieces themselves were nothing new unless one counted the ways in which one could be so highlighted in front of millions of viewers. Though basically a local story, it had developed a national appeal; even foreign countries seemed interested in the rise and fall of Florence Orville, a.k.a. Miss Dragonheel, a top---*the* top employee at the Blanchstone Agency, who had been found out to be a person of the African persuasion. Boy, nothing can create a stir like race can! But really, they shouldn't have been so shocked and retaliatory about it, after all, the days when one could have kept her out the doors were long gone, her family's ferocity of pride and rearing had all been proven a sham, and they really should have known they would be in need of a little color long ago. She hadn't *lied*, after all---she just *hadn't told them*---that was the trouble they had. They had been the surrogate family---her surrogate family---for a couple of decades, longer than her biological one had been.

And yet, now that she had examined the whole thing less partially and with some distance, she realized to her resigned disappointment that she had been no more accepted at Blanchstone than she had been by her blood relatives, only her uncanny success for the agency had kept her there, and when the chips went down hard, even that no longer mattered. Well, from then on she would rely only on herself and her own judgement. Time to do all she had been prevented from doing before for lack of time or so-called *proper* edicts. Her now-regular trips up her tree symbolized her long-lost freedom, and she devoted the subsequent year to that freedom, paying little attention to the boycotts and pickets on her behalf that still ringed the Blanchstone main offices in San Francisco. Now that her spectacle had made way for the next news topic of interest---she had not been particularly cooperative with inquirers, displaying that Miss Dragonheel temperament (or a caricature of such) to the hilt, and the Agency was no closer to hiring her back than it had been the moment they'd "placed Ms. Orville on a *leave-of-absence...*" How ironic---she had lost both *familias* for the same and yet opposite reasons. Shunned by one and shafted by the other, now she was on her own in seclusion, going out only when she wished to---or *had* to (annoying as that latter one was).

She examined her face in the mirror of her downstairs bathroom, with the fine-toothed care of a quasi-doctor. The bruises from that tipsy night beating had already faded almost to nothing, didn't look like any permanent marking had occurred. Luckier than she deserved to be, much unlike her even now to get herself drunk and pick a fight with some fool "militants." Must be some of that pesky nostalgia for them *good ole days*. Should've known better than that, lady. Suppose Dashiki Drab had seen you staggering home beat up like that! But it had been delightful to poke holes in those balloons, even though it resulted in getting some pokes of her own. *Hah! Told you not to go around thinking so good of yourself DIDN'T I! Your whiteass devil self think you're so*---Shut up. *That* was no more---from family, *or* the Agency. Her allegiance was to none, two strikes and no need for a third. No scars? Good. That'd show 'em all.

But it still could be lone.

You have no messages.

"So much for that," Florence said to herself as she mildly slammed the receiver down. "So much for the notion of taking a boarder. No sense renewing the ad.

"Probably got found out," she continued. "Or maybe it's the area, not exactly the most attractive of areas these days. To be honest, I'm no longer sure what I saw here when I bought this abode in the Miss Dragonheel days…maybe it was my way of displaying the domesticy long (and *thankfully!*) denied me. Even made sure I had an edge and wasn't backyarded by much. Somehow the margins don't seem so bad; maybe it's just being the 'whiteass' child of Garveyites.

"Oh I ramble too much," she reproached herself, snapping into action. "Time for a drive into fresh air for you, Orville!" She rushed to a closet to find a coat for traveling out this day.

Three

Florence could not help but notice the large, dark man seated on a bus bench across from her regular shopping place; he had been present for the past couple of weeks, large notepad in one hand and some sort of pencil or pen (she was too far away to see which well) in the other. He was clearly doodling something in that notepad, every so often looking at the scene ahead of him. She could not from her vantage point determine his expression to any great extent, but she had had a feeling that his view was that of a fairly scornful critic, a feeling which touched something within her as if it might have been her he was looking at. Previously she had ignored it as she continued her shopping, and did so on this day as well, but on her way out, as she was placing her purchases in the Civic, something in her had had enough. Abruptly slamming the door shut, she stalked her way to the spot where he was, crossing the street to face (and fix) him. *A stalker aimed at me hmmm? Well this prey ain't gonna fall that easy.*

She stood there over him, noting that his drawings were of the buildings in the area. They appeared accurate enough, but there was a skeletal emptiness in them, as though---well, if they had been meat parts, the bones remaining after the rest was consumed might have something in common with the buildings as rendered by this street artist.

"A most unusual depiction of your surroundings," she burst in as soon as he seemed to have completed the last piece. He turned to look up at her, but in such a composed way that she could tell she hadn't succeeded in jolting him.

"What's the cliché," he replied, "*I call them as I see them.*"

"Well then," she remarked, "how would you call *me*, for example?"

"You think I've been staring at you."

Florence instinctively opened her mouth to retort, but he went on resignedly. "Well, maybe I have and maybe I haven't. Either way, you could get the police on me and I'd end up a statistic for police abuse. Occupational hazard of being my hue and size. But maybe you have other plans."

"No, no," she said, a little jarred. "I'm neither accusing you nor trying to pick you up."

"Didn't really think so," he said, flipping a page in his notepad. "But let me try to answer your question." To her surprise, he began to sketch her quickly, looking at her off and on as he did so. Florence held still to be cooperative, not quite certain of what he was up to. Within a short time he had finished, and handed the sketch to her.

"Here you are."

She examined the sketch of herself. It was an accurate enough (albeit art deco-influenced) portrait of her face, but something about it unnerved her. The expression, while placid, had a pained, questioning air to it, as if dogged with uncertainty. Was this her mirror image? She wanted to deny that it was, but she could not take her eyes or heart away from the portrait. *Looks like you've got lots yet to learn.*

"You've...got quite a talent," she said.

"Even I can use one," he replied.

"This is something I would like to look over. You don't mind if---?" She moved to dig inside her purse.

"Not at all. You can keep it...and the money too."

"Then would you at least sign it?" she asked, offering the portrait back to him. He took it, scribbled in it at its lower right corner, then returned it to her.

"Thanks---very much."

"No problem."

She made her way back to the Civic, a little humbled in embarrassment over what she had prejudged. It was not exactly clear to her how she had managed to avoid colliding with something, for her eyes were on the portrait.

But it was only after she was inside and secured herself in preparation to leave that she realized what had been written on the portrait.

To my idol the legendary Miss Dragonheel---Breed Hamilton.

She hissed. *Why that manipulative---!*

Yet she was not sure whether it was out of anger or a gesture of a touché.

Four

A few hours later, after dropping off and putting away her groceries at her place, she stood at a lookout point in the hills that she occasionally went to, looking out at the panoramic view of the sun setting over the Golden Gate. To think that this was once her oyster of sorts---that she could, perhaps even had, conquered the world and smote dead those who had put her down, designated her as a reminder of who knew how many rapings of who knew how many great aunts, grandmothers or whatever. Hell, she hadn't even asked to be that reminder, let alone the one that had shamed her fiercely-proud parents and given birth to the very "devil" they despised---her. But since those fiercely-proud relations had constantly accused her of being some witch with special powers possessed by light-skinned women and special privileges granted her by the grand inquisitor society for which they had cast her out as some sort of aberration---a stain upon the family's nationalist honor. Well, those powers and privileges had served her well in the climb to power and empowerment. Too bad the bottom fell out when the Blanchstone Agency had learned the truth. Yep, those powers and privileges had served her *real* well.

In the times immediately following the termination when she had come up here, it would have been all too easy to walk forward and jump into the air, bringing this life of hers to closure. But then that would have only satisfied them all, and no way was she about to do that!

And now even had she still been inclined to do so, this trip the picture drawn of her was stuck in her mind, unable---un*willing* to free itself. Damn it would have been easier had she simply left everything alone and remained at least comfortable with visions of dark vulgarity. But stubborn her, she just had to meet and conquer. That time she was conquered. Well, *Mister* Breed Hamilton, sooner or later there *will* be a round two! Much appreciated sir.

She turned towards where she had parked the Civic. Enough gazing at what might have been.

Five

She was driving too fast through the curves and hills. Really, she would have to watch that. But it would be so hard---this was one of the few means of power she had left, other than her house, and she could hardly move *that*.

She casually glanced at her watch somewhere along the trip. *Oh! didn't realize it was that late!* "That's what you get for being such a leadfoot," she mock-scolded herself as she hooked into the next turnoff.

A few minutes downward she noted some sort of commotion ahead, slowing up so as to get a glimpse of what the fuss was about and to avoid accidentally hitting someone should they get rowdy enough to jolt out in her path. It was a frantic chase; a mob of about a dozen was shouting obscenities at the object of their chase. It was a large black male, which somehow raised Florence's ire. *So that's who you're chasing! Act like South will you!*

Abruptly flooring the accelerator, she rocketed past the startled mob and their prey, and jerked right just ahead of the latter, cutting him off but kicking the door facing him open.

"*Get in---quick!*" she cried at him, and he instinctively threw himself inside, whereupon she floored it again as he quickly shut the door, leaving the frustrated and angry mob to sulk and loudly curse as one. It had all happened too fast for anyone to even get a glimpse at the car or its license.

When Florence finally turned to face the man she had rescued, her face froze briefly, for she recognized him.

"Looks like we meet again, Miss Dragonheel," Breed replied.

"No need to call me that," she remarked with quick composure. "Those days are gone now, might as well call me Florence like everyone else. But what were you doing out there?"

"Well, Florence, we flatland folk like to visit the views too. Least some of us do." He grunted as though to get serious. "Trouble was, I missed the last bus while delivering a portrait to someone 'round here, and as I was trudging through there ran into some clowns who didn't like my portraits and liked my—*our*---kind even less." He paused. "Along with my dark hue and perceived class."

"Yeah, some utopia this turned out to be," she found herself having to agree. "But didn't you realize how late it was?"

"Not when I do my work," he said, reaching into his pack and pulling out several pictures.

"Can't look at them right now---wait'll we stop off."

"Oh, I wasn't offering them, only trying to examine them." He looked through his work. "Good---the ruckus didn't mess up any of them."

"I ought to charge you for this ride," she joshed. "You *do* owe me one, Mr. Hamilton."

"Might as well call me Breed like everyone else," he smiled wryly. "Considering it all, I'm rather lucky."

"*You're* lucky I don't kick you," she mock-snapped. "Breed."

Six

"O-*kay*, here you are---Breed Hamilton's place to stay, everyone off," Florence teased.

"Thanks very much for everything," Breed said as he exited the car, clutching his pictures, pack and coat.

"Decent pictures too, from what little I could glance at while driving. Couldn't risk wrecking myself with you about."

"I appreciate what you've done...I *do* owe you, Florence."

"How true. But I warn you, that may come back to haunt you. 'Bye," she said, waving to him as he closed the car door.

He waved back to her as she began to drive off.

Ahhh shit there he is as usual that black power outage. She was not looking forward to dealing with Dashiki Drab at this late hour; all she wanted was to get her hide home. But obviously that was not to be. *Does he never take a break!*

Sure enough as soon as she had set foot out of her car there he was. "*You do know woman! It's time to join the battle---leave the bourgeois prison behind and join in the glory of the Nubian diaspora you poor misled African queen---*"

"Get lost," she grumbled without looking at him as she clicked her way to her Italianate Villa and unlocked the door to let herself in.

But he stood on the sidewalk facing though not following her, and continued as though he had not heard her. "*---remember what Malcolm the Great said BY ANY MEANS NECESSARY the descendants of Garvey will rise and take us away from this wretched land and return us to our true motherland---*"

She slammed the door behind her. Jackass---Garvey would never have had her anyway, she knew *that* much. She could still hear him ranting on and loud as he moved on. Let him go run himself down---what'd she care; see if she did.

She stomped up the stairs, more in haughty defiance than anxiety or anger, taking pride in each step she made in her very own place. Though this had been hers for years, her pride, in a curious way, was one of having just bought her own home bare minutes ago. And *this* nobody could take away like they had her job.

She could hear the collective *Aw-w-w-w-w!* of foiled oppressors at that fact as she turned towards her bedroom.

Lying on her bed, she imagined herself strapped to it, her wrists and ankles struggling beneath unreal ropes. Spread-eagled on her back, it was all she could do to move her head up enough to see the parliament of dark stern bodies in black staring in cold judgment of her. On either side stood a sister and a brother and between the two sets were the mother and father---no, not the biological father (at least not of *her*), just the mother's husband. She stared at this jury with defiance that, though genuine, belied a childlike appeal which after all the years still refused to stay away. A recurring dream? Or nightmare? Was this really of her making---or just another of her adventures or fairy tale of her own creation?

Thought you could flee us did you? Well you little tainted miss we got your unclean ass now you like having your paleass legs exposed when you're in your trees maybe you'll learn yourself confined to this bed the rest of YOUR LIFE YOUR LIFE---

"Wrong again worthless fools clinging to your god your *GAWD* who didn't even leave a tangible legacy blaming me for your disgrace I didn't ask for this mixing up of bloodlines---"

HUSH YOUR MOUTH when you speak of HIM OF HIM OF HIM OF HIM---

She somehow snapped the straps binding her ankles, raised her legs as she brought them together-*--Oh he can't save you now he never was good at actually SAVING anyone was he!*---and once her legs were between the parents she abruptly jerked them apart, splitting the mob in half to reveal a large, tall white male in a Southern colonel's suit, grinning gruffly as though the actions were a charade and he was impressed by the show.

So blind you are you don't even realize who the real cause of your disgrace is---the cause that knew your renown and did his number on mother poor you and created the disgrace and laughing stock you presume you lost when you yanked me by my hair and threw me out

NONONONOOOYOUDIDYOUDIDYOUDII IIIIIDDDDDDDD!!!!!!!!!!!

Oh go away.

She rose up to a seated position on her bed, triumphant and free of bonds, real or imaginary. Even part naked in bedclothes, they could not bring back the former bastard who had so glaringly reminded them of the futility of Nubian pride. This was, after all, Miss Dragonheel.

Now and still.

"Now I've no excuse to ignore Mr. Hamilton's works," she mused. "Done wiped out my sleep."

Seven

Breed Hamilton sat at the battered makeshift desk in his room, cluttered and rather too small for one of his size, finishing up some sketches and words. The day had been quite eventful for him, and though it was earlier than when he usually went to bed, the toll had started to tire him prematurely. But it had not quelled the fire that dwelt within him as he nursed and savored the memory of having met the one and only Miss Dragonheel, Florence Orville---*Finally!*---after the interest he had had in her through her sad story of her fall from power as the top agent of the Blanchstone Agency.

Finishing up the last of his sketches, he put them away for the evening, then turned to a nearby box and began to pull out his Miss Dragonheel paraphernalia, consisting primarily of newspaper clippings and magazine articles, but also with a few pictures and even some satirical drawings from a few papers, and eye them with care, as though looking through cherished archives. He himself had never caricatured Florence in any of his sketches--- somehow that seemed to him to be rather mocking of her situation. He felt a kinship with her to a degree, ever since the story first broke out, and was awed at having now met her despite a feeling that he was entering the den of a very hungry lioness; she had warned as much to him, and he knew she could indeed chew him up and spit out his remains, all the while holding him in ecstasy. Yet even with that this situation was by no means the eggshell he had known from his budding years, the ones in which he had *really* had to watch his step for fear of never making another. He speculated within himself that Florence had had similar experiences in her childhood, though the two were obviously years apart there.

After a little while examining his collection, he put it away. Undressing himself, he was about to place himself into bed when a gentle rap came upon his door. Though it was a most inopportune time, he rose up without annoyance, in part because he knew there was only one person it could possibly be, who would do that (only one person often did that anytime), and even had there been many friends, this one would always be welcome in his heart. He only gazed through the peephole as a reflex action while he opened the door.

"Good evening, Breed." The soft warmth of her voice always gave him novel assurance even after almost two years' tenancy here.

"Welcome to tonight's rendition, Bianca," he joshed quietly, holding the door open to let her inside. That royal yet gentle stride of hers was always kind viewing for him, as was the smooth rustle of the off-white evening dress that shaped and elongated her already statuesque figure, still quite fit even though she was of comparable age to Florence (who also belied her age, albeit in her own way). The sharp serenity of her face was augmented by the slender red lips, rouge and shadow (not that her face truly needed such) and topped by the elegant, blond-streaked brown hair. In a sense she was rather inappropriate for the clutter of the room, even if it (along with the house) was legally hers.

He suddenly realized he was almost nude save for his underpants. "*Oh---!---*I'm sorry for this---I was just getting ready---"

"No need for apology," she reassured with a mild laugh. "I've seen quite a few like that before; you go right on ahead."

He did, getting himself into the bed, feigning oblivion to her presence. Bianca, aware of his apprehension, feigned oblivion as well. As soon as he was secure in the bed, she moved toward him and sat herself on it beside him, caressing him with one hand.

"So...done any new masterpieces lately?"

"They're on the table."

"Let's see," she replied, reaching out to the table and grasping the pile of sketches on it, then looking them over with an inquiring yet supportive eye. "You seem quite fixed on Florence Orville tonight."

"I met her this afternoon."

"You did...? Bet *that* was much the surprise!"

"It was...and not only did I meet her, she also took some of my portraits of her---and I even got my hide saved by Miss Dragonheel herself!"

"Three in one day!" Bianca exclaimed. "How many people would kill for that."

"I know," Breed said. "It all seems so...ethereal, for lack of a better term. Ever since that scandal about her, I've felt this kinship...and now, running into her...it all seems like two cultural exiles."

"I think I have an idea of what you're getting at," she nodded. "You see some of you in her."

"I guess so..." he replied. "But it's strange. I've never obsessed on any one person before I learned of her, and now that I've actually met her..."

"*So-o-o*---it would appear, Mr. Hamilton," Bianca teased, "you've got a crush on Miss Florence Orville!"

He instinctively shot up to a sit-up position. "Now that's---ridiculous!" he shot in embarrassment. "If I had a crush on *anyone,* it'd be you!"

"At ease, my dear," she smiled, easing him back down with her upper body. "I'm not jealous. Besides, you're only defensive because I'm in a sense providing your room and board. As a matter of fact---" She moved her face so it was directly looking down at his. "---I hope there's room for a third cultural exile."

"If it's you," he said, "there'll be plenty of room." He paused as though coming to an uneasy realization. "But what of your family?"

"*I'll* worry about that, *dulce* Breed," she remarked with a confidence that warmed him, despite his apprehension. "Meanwhile, I'll give you a 'crush' of my own." Shifting her body over his, she embraced him tightly. Breed took in her body's warmth and pressure, which he never could suppress his ecstasy for.

"Satisfied now?" she murmured after several minutes.

"You've got me," he admitted, "as always, Dona Bianca."

"Thought so." She kissed his cheek. "Goodnight, Breed, and enjoy your sleep." With that, she rolled herself off him to her feet, and, as

Breed watched, blew a kiss to him as she turned out the light. Not long afterwards he was fast asleep.

"More portraits of me," Florence mused to herself as she examined Breed's pictures with a skeptical eye. She sat a diva's cross-legged posture on the armchair in her living room, still in nightwear, looking over the pictures he had left her.

"Head shot of me looking bold---medium focus of myself---looks like the day I first saw him in that parking lot...profile shot...questing look...*hmmm*---oh! Now *that* beats all! A superheroine rendition of Miss Dragonheel!" She had to laugh at that. "*Defender of human dignity against the forces who would destroy human compassion---*"

A loud guffaw burst from her throat. She set down the pictures, unable to keep them stable in her amusement. "*Boy you must've got your info about me through some drunk!*" she remarked before she slapped a hand over her mouth as though she had said a bad word. But to her it was almost as obscene.

"And after all these years too---!" she gasped softly. Even now that primitive voice still came out of her. *Damn!* thought she had long conquered *that* when she'd joined forces with the Blanchstone Agency. Maybe---now that the ties were forever severed---could the primitive be now encroaching upon her without that firm's protection? Could the *family* be exacting its revenge?

She turned to the pile of pictures (the one of the superheroine Miss Dragonheel on top) with a glare. Don't you go gloating you displays of Breed. You made me burst like that and I'll show you what it means to catch Miss Dragonheel unawares. But first---I'll need the best of rest after all. Good night---but tomorrow I shall fix you but good.

Foolish woman. Pictures can't make you do a thing; thing is, this Breed Hamilton's on to you. A stalker, maybe? No, somehow that didn't seem quite Breed. But it would be kind of interesting anyway---certainly I've not gotten so much attention devoted to me elsewhere.

Rambling too much. I *do* need rest.

She rose to her feet and stretched, only to realize she had not the energy to attempt a climb upstairs. *S'okay---my house---no law against using the couch.*

And she did, after turning out the light and sinking into her couch.

Her eyes opened to reveal the warmth of sunrays upon her, having penetrated the windows and the curtains covering them. On instinct she reached for one of several remote controls and grasped at empty air. It was then that she remembered she was in her living room and not her bedroom where her more up-to-date technology was.

"Of course there's a TV here too," she observed for no particular reason, "but it's got no inkling of what would come a decade or so after it came along." She forced herself wearily into a sit-up position. "Much like its owner," she added as she rubbed her eyes. With a quiet yawn, she rose to her feet and moved up the stairs to her bedroom and the day's preparations---one of which would qualify as an irritation.

Eight

"Now look," the doctor said with vacuous paternity, "you *are* obviously an intelligent, perhaps even *brilliant*, woman, and can write your own ticket despite this...*de-cept-ion*...of yours; indeed, you maintained one for many years, no dumb filly could've pulled *that* off---" He smiled at his own words. "---*but*---"

"---but you just can't seem to get it through your head that this medication is good for you," Florence droned in exact unison with him.

"Good for stupor and drool," she remarked in resigned defiance, laid up on her back in exaggerated agony on the psychiatrist's couch.

"I swear, Miss Orville, you seem to want me to discontinue this relationship. You remember, do you not, that I *am* one of a pathetically few to remain with you despite everything when your game was exposed."

"Congratulations, my dear doctor," she mock-beamed. Just your luck, Orville---least most of the others at Blanchstone of the City were open about it---no doubt about their honesty.

"And you're always passing up the opportunity to relax here as well," the doctor continued. "You're not so young a lass anymore, Miss Orville, and those flawed genes of yours can use a rest."

"I had a good night's sleep," she replied dryly. And that *flawed genes* remark ain't nothing worth no small reply---*oops*---watch it, woman.

"You don't know about that," the doctor replied.

She gave one loud guffaw at that, but knew better than to speak, for her lingo would have slipped out as it had the previous night. It was during a time of such urges that she wondered if she was becoming a split or multiple personality. But she was not about to give this still-pimply company man the satisfaction of inquiring about *that* possibility.

"Look," she finally said, sitting up, "you mustn't think I'm not at all grateful for your philanthropy---" (*Though goodness knows I'm NOT, you cub scout!*) "---but surely you must have other patients in need of your hard-earned and most prodigious expertise. What say you give me your prescription and let me go armed with your compassion so you can stay in good with the others?"

"Why, how considerate of you, Miss Orville!" the doctor beamed as if *he* had thought up the idea. "And in anticipation of your need---" He reached into a desk-drawer and pulled out a small sheet of paper and handed it to Florence, who rose to her feet in perfect timing to his gesture. "---I took the precaution of having your prescription typed up in advance."

"Oh thank you, doctor," she murmured. "Good luck with the other patients."

"Good day, Miss Orville," he said as Florence closed the door behind her.

Walking through the hall on the way to the elevators, Florence looked over the prescription and muttered the contents rapidly under her breath. When she was at the elevators, she pressed the down button, then backed herself a few feet to become parallel with a receptacle with a pedal-operated lid. She waited. Then---

The down light button turned off.

Florence's foot pressed the receptacle's pedal.

Her hand crumpled the prescription paper---

(The bell signaled the elevator's arrival.)

---and opened up, dropping the paper's remains into the receptacle.

Her foot released the receptacle's pedal, closing its lid shut.

And she stalked casually towards and into the opened elevator.

Nine

"---*well ha-ha-ha---who's got the last laugh now-w-w-w---*"

She felt a love-hate hypnotic lure to that thirties song; she always did when hearing it as she was on the radio on her way back to her place, ever since one day a little over a decade ago, when she had by then cemented her reputation at the Blanchstone Agency and rocked the world as the legendary Miss Dragonheel. She had just received a telegram with what should have been tragic news---*MOTHER DEAD*. She had not even pretended to feel much remorse over that---how could she have done so? Had that not been the woman who had regularly vented her rage on this child of a violation which had smashed all pretense of the black empowerment that she and her husband had reveled in and which had been continued through the years since their proud Jamaican icon had been driven from the US of A? The woman who had savagely knocked her down with a slap to her daughter's face, screaming insanities upon hearing the news of the attempted rape of that daughter by another prominent whitey. *Slut! Heathen child! Bastard whiteass heifer! Think you can have anything well here's this and THIS AND THIS GET OUT OUT OUTTTTTTTTTTTTTTT!!!!!!!!!!!!* The memory of the impacted ground she had landed on and the near-ripping out of her hair, coupled with the stony, condemning look of the always distant never intervening husband through her blurred, tearful (and in one case, blackened) eyes, had still haunted her even decades later.

That had been the last time she had had contact with any of them. Yet even so, even after she had been taken in by a white couple who was sympathetic to the black struggle and who had recently lost a daughter (quite possibly seeing her as a surrogate; all that had mattered to the young and traumatized Florence was finding someone to protect her and to answer what would now become of her), and becoming all that she could become, in fact was just about at the peak of her powers by then---she had tried to contact them, with no success.

The telegram had needed some payment. She had been so relieved she paid the deliveryman double the cost and insisted he take it all. Then, after he had gone, she turned on a stereo system in her living room and had heard the first bars of *They All Laughed*. Without intending to she had danced in wild merriment and sang loudly to the chorus *"Well ha-ha-ha, who's got the last laugh now!"*

After the song was finished she had turned off the stereo system and threw herself triumphantly on her couch, as though she had just returned from a very grand gala. *My, that was quite a---mourning!* She could not help giggling giddily as though she was slightly drunk. But she had been aware that she had not reacted in any such way upon learning of the death of her mother's husband a few years earlier---or of her father's some years before that--- the father who had never known prosecution for his actions. Sexism? Racism? Or simply the final end to a terrible trio?

That had been a little over a decade ago, during which she had made no further attempts to contact any of her blood relatives. They knew where she was if any of them wished to contact or reconcile with her. Their absence and silence was the answer to any questions one dared inquire her about forgiveness or reconciliation.

And that was saying nothing about any contact attempt on their part during the scandal.

Despite herself, Florence was beginning to develop an interest in Breed. If he was not at the house where she had dropped him off the other night, he might be in one of his working grounds, doing his sketches---*no doubt some of which are of me!* He seemed so vulnerable to her, and she was beginning to wonder if she was forming a maternal instinct towards him. (*Me, a mother figure at this late date---haw!*)

Still, it couldn't hurt to check up on him. "Besides," she said to herself, "he still owes me!"

Taking her usual exit off the freeway, she turned not in the direction of her house, but towards the area where she had usually found him doing his sketches.

But Breed was not to be found, at least not anywhere in his familiar haunts, much to Florence's chagrin. She had first stopped by the house where he resided, but he had already left for the day. Then she had driven by the places she had seen him sketching, but this day there was no sign of him. She had even considered driving to the area in the hills where she had rescued him from the mob, but decided he'd not be brave or foolish enough to venture in that particular place for a good long while.

After about twenty minutes of searching, she decided to return home and hope he was simply doing a change of pace activity. This city was much too large to look all over it (assuming he was in the city at all!), and she was a little tired from the psychiatrist's appointment. "I really *must* get myself a real psychotherapist," she muttered to herself.

"But hopefully I won't have to get myself a new Breed."

"The call is for YOU, Florence Orville! For you to abandon this game and come home to the greatness of your people!"

Just her luck. No luck in finding Breed, plenty of luck in finding that Dashiki Drab. She was in no mind to deal with his mouthings today, after the charade with her doctor and the lack of success in locating Breed to at least thank him ("Not that I would *ever* be in any mood to deal with *him* anyway," she grumbled to herself, referring to Dashiki Drab). At times it seemed that the world was out to deprive her of friends and give her all kinds of troublesome fools.

"*Return HOME, Florence Orville!*" Dashiki Drab roared. "*RETURN to the roots that bore and nurtured you. Return...*"

She marched herself inside, fed up with the day even though it was mid-afternoon.

Ten

"*Awww-w-w-w couldn't find your lone friend on this earth?*" the man in the white Southern colonel's suit taunted the infuriated Florence, who was below him scaling up a very steep cliffside, above which he stood ogling her, twirling his hat. "*That's what these things called friends can do to you...why not go back to the FAM-I-LEE...like...ME!! Hahahahaha---*"

"*You hornyass PERVERT!*" she hissed with rage, exhaustion and frustration in inching her way up and keeping her footing. "*Run to you---I'll SPIT on you!*"

"*On your own Pater?*" he remarked in mock-disappointment. "*Tsk tsk...you poor little despicable half-nigger tree-climbing orphan.*" And with those words, all the more infuriating to Florence for their genteel tone, he abruptly flung his hat at her, its brim impacting square onto her nose. She gave an involuntary roar, more from surprise than pain, and lost her hold.

She felt herself tumbling and rolling downwards...

"Well, that wasn't one of my finer hours!" Florence exclaimed to herself from her lopsided, sprawled position towards the bottom of her stairway.

She was not clear exactly on how long she had lain there, still as if not moving at all, even to straighten her position to at least an upright one, would disrupt some sort of order or whatever. Her position caused her to glimpse in her mind that of the hapless teacher in *The Birds* after the title characters had done her in---though Florence was sprawled on a narrower and steeper stairway, indoors and obviously not dead except for her career---bruised a little in a few places (*Ain't you getting on for this, honey!*) but by no means ready to be daisy food. *Please don't be ate by the daisies.*

A ringing sound.

"The phone..?" she mused, almost making it a question, then gasped as if just now realizing where she was. "*Crap!* What're you doing lying there, Orville, someone---*one person*---wants you!" And she struggled and rolled and forced herself up with considerable effort ("Oh how the villains would laugh seeing their adversary like this!" she moaned). No time to unite her shoes, one lying midway on a stair and the other on the floor below---she had a duty to do, anxieties to cure ("And a way to find out why I'm sounding like Breed's rendition of Miss Dragonheel!" she exclaimed to herself).

Alighting precisely at her telephone, she picked it up. "Hello---who is it?"

"Florence---"

"*Breed!*" (*That was a little too breathtaking for you, Florence!*) Resisting the urge to demand *Where were you!*, she modified her tone. "How nice to call. What've you been up to?"

"I took the day off---did the town of sorts with Bianca---"

"Bianca---?"

"Oh, I've not mentioned her...she's a patron of mine."

"She's familiar with your work, I take it."

"Yeah," Breed said. "She wants to meet you---we'd thought to visit, but didn't know if you'd be home or not. I realize it's short notice, but---"

"No problem," Florence replied. "I'd be glad to meet this Bianca, she sounds like someone most interesting." *I've barely heard of the woman and I'm already saying she's interesting! Still, the company should quench my hunger.* "Listen, if you can give me a bit of time I might be able to fix something up...just a snack or something, okay?"

"If it's no trouble."

"It's *not*, I assure you." *Not so defensive, woman!* "Give me about an hour, alright?"

"That should be fine. We'll see you then."

"Looking forward to it."

"*Well*, Florence Orville," she said to herself after hanging up, "that wasn't one person but *two* wanting you. Parents cry in your graves---all three stooges of you. While I straighten myself up."

Moving to the stairway, she picked up her shoes. "Now I'm June Cleaver," she mused as she put them on, "only without the pearls and with darker and longer hair. And now, for the kitchen to see what I have." And that was the room she entered.

"No Beaver, no Wally---or even a Ward," she added as though just remembering that element, as she opened her refrigerator to see what was available.

Eleven

When Florence saw Dona Bianca San Cortez to the right of Breed upon answering and opening her front door she could understand what he saw in her, as a feeling rocketed within her that this may well be the closest thing to royalty she was likely to see at her doorstep. "A tall woman, this Bianca," she observed whimsically to herself, "and what an aura! No wonder he sings her praises...she obviously means the world to him!"

"Good evening," she said, "and come on in. Dinner's not much---"(*especially since I neglected to ask what you liked fool me!*) "---but it should pass and it's almost ready."

"Thank you for inviting us," Bianca said, greeting Florence with a handshake. "You must be Florence, the legendary Miss Dragonheel---Breed's talked much of you."

"*Too flattering,*" Florence said to herself as she shot a fixing glare at Breed. "I didn't realize I'd talked about myself that much," she said to her guests. "But I'd rather not talk *too* much about me at the moment."

"Well, you're the host," Bianca remarked.

"But I would like to find out a bit more of you," Florence continued. "Breed's very lucky to have you there for him---" A small bell rang, and she shrugged apologetically. "---but it looks like I'll have to wait to find that out. That was the sound of the readiness of dinner." She rushed to her kitchen to see to the final preparations, calling out "It's okay for you two to go to the table---I'll be out shortly!"

Bianca turned to Breed. "I guess we should head over to the table."

"Indeed," he replied, not quite knowing of anything better to say due to his overall nervousness.

The elaboration of the dinner menu was still holding Breed in some surprise when Florence finally joined him and Bianca at the table. Though clearly portioned for three, the number of items suggested a party for many more. A main course, drinks, appetizers and desserts ringed the table's center, and the aromas and atmosphere seemed to suggest a surprisingly high-class café. Either Florence was in a really generous mood, he thought, or she was attempting to make up for lost time (in terms of lost opportunities to host get-togethers). Or both.

"Thought you were having many guests for awhile," he said jokingly to her when she arrived to take her place.

"Oh no," she replied as delightfully demure as she could relish, "why not the best for good people!"

The dinner conversation was somewhat routine as far as Florence's getting more acquainted with her guests and they with her was concerned. At some point in the conversation the topic turned to Bianca's background, and specifically concerning her husband. Florence noted a slight change in the atmosphere but thought better of bringing up that; for all she knew, it may simply have been an unpleasant memory of sorts.

"---well," Bianca said to her, "my husband engaged in diplomatic work, related to the ambassador. Was much honored at it..." She paused. "...but he's dead now."

"Oh..." Florence gasped in a whisper, thinking that it had happened quite recently (or possibly under extremely traumatic circumstances). "I'm very sorry..."

"Still," Bianca continued, "even nine years later, I just can't stop thinking of him at times...have you ever been married?"

"No. But I can imagine how losing someone as close to you as you---" (*WHOA Florence! you almost said "you two."*) "---and your husband must have been to each other." (*Liar Florence!*)

"Anyhow," Bianca said, "with my husband gone and the children off and flown from the nest, I thought of taking in a boarder."

"*A boarder!*" Florence exclaimed to herself but did not dare to say aloud. "*Some folks have all the luck---boy am I jealous!*"

"Was that how you and Breed met?" she did inquire out loud.

"Oh, no---no," Breed and Bianca said together, unintentionally.

"She had---another boarder when I first met her," Breed elaborated. "He was a sculptor, but was starting to really hit big---in fact, it was at a reception for one of his exhibits that we met, and, as it turns out, at...just...the right time..." He trailed off and hung his head, as Bianca clutched his hand with her own in sympathy. Florence, looking on at this, felt something ring inside her as she viewed this, well aware that this was not a pleasant reminiscence for him, and that this may not be his most unpleasant memory.

"Do you want to stop...?" Bianca whispered to him. "I can continue for you if..."

"No, that's all right...all right," he said, shaking his head and steeling himself. "In any case, things at the board-and-care were getting out of hand---" ("*No doubt about your art,*" *Florence thought to herself*) "---and the sculptor was ready to move on, so---a couple of weeks later he did, and a week after that, I moved into Bianca's place."

"If you're aware of the aficionados of---say, the arts, serving as patron, benefactor, or---simply offering lodging and a place to relax of sorts from the ravages of the world," Bianca said, "well, Florence, that's sort of been my role for the past number of years."

"A most interesting role," Florence said for want of something more complex to say.

"We actually started taking boarders when my husband was alive," Bianca went on, "after the children had left, but after he died soon after---it's taken a whole new sense of urgency for me." She looked at Florence as though a bit embarrassed by what she had to say next. "You might say one boarder leaves and another comes soon to take his place."

Florence could only nod in understanding.

"Fortunately," Bianca continued, "money's no real problem for me---my husband and I had made some wise investments and gotten some really good insurance---" She stopped briefly as if wanting to choose her next words carefully. "---all other concerns are minimal rather."

Florence had some twist of suspicion that this was not exactly the complete truth, but as Bianca's concern for Breed was clearly genuine and devoid of any deception, and she herself came off as quite sincere and even admirable, she did not feel obliged to press the matter further. She turned to Breed, who was just finishing his meal. "So, how's the food been for you?"

"Been very good," he replied. "I for one appreciate your effort."

"Nothing at all," she smiled, somehow unable to resist the urge to be a seen-it-all warm cynic.

Twelve

Florence finished the last of the cleanup after the visit with her guests. It had been quite refreshing to have someone over at her home again after all this period of near-isolation. Took her mind off her own troubles and concerns of which she had been focusing too much on. Breed and Bianca made a rather handsomely quaint---if a tad offbeat---tandem.

"A most relieving party of sorts," she mused, "and best of all, I learned that my skills at hosting haven't atrophied one bit---only the numbers of guests have!

"But now," she continued, "that the meal and the conversing have concluded (and admirably so, I might add!), the cloaks of loneliness and uncertainty---" Pausing, she looked up as though speaking to someone above. "---threaten to envelope yours truly in its maw---enveloped---in the *maw!*" She laughed at the irony of words.

Thirteen

ONE TIME RISING STAR DION HAPLESS
COMMITS APPARENT SUICIDE AT AGE 35.
"*---and one of Hapless' most notorious
episodes was the controversial split with his agent,
Florence Orville, top agent of the Blanchstone
Agency, citing that Orville had tormented and
forced him to cast aside his racially-conscious
'real' name for a more 'proper' name and stardom
years ago when he was nineteen. Some sources
consider it ironic that a decade later Orville herself
was exposed as a light-skinned African-American.*

"And that was Miss Dragonheel for you,"
Florence sighed, wiping a tear from her eye as she
sadly released the newspaper from her fingers the
following morning. Slumped in her easy chair, she
watched it plop with a rustle to the floor. "No doubt
many others agree with poor Mister Hapless about
the legacy and bruised wake of Miss Dragonheel,
even though most didn't necessarily allow it...to
give her the satisfaction of seeing them end it all.
Who knows...maybe even as recent as last week I
might've casually shrugged it off as an individual
failing. What a petulantly horrific thought that is
now."

"So---you're *not* so happy about my demise
after all," a voice mocked in her ear as if the source
had been in conversation with and beside her.

She recognized the voice. Looking up, she
almost rose up in alarm, for there he was, tall, thin
and a bit hang doggish of the face, almost as fair as
hers, though despite his having been roughly a
decade her junior, he looked nearly twice her age.

The face, always with a forlorn demeanor, seemed much more so now.

"Why Miss Orville---Miss *Dragonheel*---you seem hurt about my latest act. Too bad it's not one I can repeat this time."

"I am hurt, yes," she admitted. "Surely nothing could have been so bad as to precipitate...this."

"Nothing, in or of itself. Not even you could do that on your own. Just everything in and all at once. But it seemed quite tempting to haunt your soul like the memories of your little badger act haunted me years after."

"I...was given bad information," she said, "and wound up passing it on to everyone under my four-inch heel."

"Yeah, I realized that," Hapless agreed, "especially after all the shit hit your fanny. At the time, I even felt sad for you...*almost*. But by then, the racial turmoil you gave me about the name---did you know how badly it broke my mother's heart? Or how angry it had made my father? Never did fully patch up with either of them; they died thinking I'd spat on all their efforts to raise me with pride. But who knows---maybe I can reconcile with them here."

"Oh, Kamil-Abdul," Florence began, not bothering to hold back her weeping, "if only---"

"*Kamil-Abdul?*" he said incredulously. "How ironic that is...*now*. But it's a bit late to cry for me, Florence---huh, this first-name stuff is catching. You know, I came here with the intention of haunting you silly...a big payback, if you will. But now I really don't have the heart---no, it's not seeing you wailing like this or knowing of your downfall. I came to seek poetic justice and wind up finding forgiveness---or as close to it as I can get now. But it's still too late to cry for me, Florence; I'm over and done with. Be thankful most of the others didn't go to my extreme, and I know for sure some of them did come real close to doing so. But it's not too late for anyone you meet in the future, or for Breed."

This jolted her into sitting up. "How do you---?"

"That's not important," Hapless said, "at least not for you. But he needs you, and you need him...far more than either of you realize. Miss Dragonheel is forever strong within you. Channel her well, and you might never be haunted with a memory like me again."

Florence blinked involuntarily, and looked to see Hapless, but she realized with a shock that she was the only person in the room.

"Dion---?" she called out.

Silence.

"Hapless---?"

Silence.

"Kamil-Abdul---?

"Had this been a hallucination? Or a *delusion?* Or sign of the gods making me mad before destroying me?" she wondered. "Oh how poetic a justice young Dion Hapless *nee* Kamil-Abdul Kwame would find that!"

Touching a hand to her face she realized it was quite soaked, and that her eyes were swollen. "So I have been crying," she observed as if she was learning she could do that for the first time.

But what had Hapless meant about Breed? And if what he said was true, what indeed of Bianca? Hapless had not mentioned her---could that mean---? She bolted to her feet, then checked herself.

"Relax, Florence," she reproved herself mildly. "Letting yourself get worked up like this, and before you've even done anything! You need to relax."

But as soon as she took her first step, she knew, bizarre as it might seem, where.

Fourteen

The ascent up the oak was a morning workout of sorts, each muscle in her body from arms to toes pulling, pushing and caressing itself into action along and against the solid wood and bark as it met the challenge over the authoritarian militia of gravity, age, gender roles and logic.

"Ah, the mighty adventure I take again," she beamed to herself as though she were conquering Mount Everest. "But it's my more pensive places I seek."

Making her way through the paths of the branches, she made her way to a group of branches that were close enough together for her to wrap herself in and look on at the ground some dozen feet or so below. Here, arms and legs locked around the main branch, she imagined herself as a she-leopard on her perch surveying all about her (though in actuality it was just her backyard). She didn't quite know how or why, but it was here that she could relax and unwind most effectively. Perhaps it was that she could finally indulge her tomboyish and other daring wiles without answering to anyone for it. "Oh how seductive this feels," she mused. "The freedom, the challenge, the *me*ness…but be careful! You could even fall asleep here---"

She heard two sets of giggling below her.

"*Oh-h-h*," she smiled, "I've got a chorus here! I won't even dare ask how they got in."

But what was down below startled her. There, scuffling almost like children (or possibly young lovers) competing with each other in horseplay, were Breed and Bianca, grappling merrily and obviously having a splendid time. Taking turns on top and on bottom, their bodies pressing against each other, they seemed happier than either they or anyone else would dare to let on in public.

"I *thought* that relationship had more to it than met the eye!" Florence delighted (but quietly so as not to disturb the two). "And if so, good for the both of you, Breed Hamilton and Dona Bianca San Cortez!"

But in the time it took for her to make that statement, Breed and Bianca had mysteriously vanished. "*Humph*---just like…*Kamil-Abdul*," she observed, rather disappointed. "But at least nothing seems to have happened badly…except maybe to my mind."

Yet she was not entirely ready to dismiss Hapless' prophecy---"these things *are* after all known to strike when one least expects it," she thought to herself as, having had her fill of her leopard's watch, she descended from the oak.

Fifteen

She watched herself press the buttons on her telephone as if she were a receptionist called to urgent duty. "Oh, I hope *somebody* is at home," she panicked.

Within a few rings the desperately-awaited click sounded.

"Hello...?" Bianca's voice.

"Bianca? It's me, Florence Orville."

"Oh!---how nice of you to call."

"And how nice of you to be there," Florence thought silently before replying out loud, "you two got home all right, it seems."

"We did indeed," Bianca said. "And meeting you was so wonderful, as was your hospitality. Thank you very much, Miss Orville."

"You're welcome. Is Breed there?"

"No; you just missed him. He's off on his art trips---doing some masterpieces, no doubt. But in a sense, Miss Orville, and you may think me a tad loco for what I'm about to suggest---"

("Not half of the loco I fear I'm stricken with," thought Florence to herself.)

"---but is it possible for you to come to my place for a little bit? I'd like to show you some of his work, other than that of you."

Ah, a promoter for Breed! "Sure, Mrs. San Cortez, I'd be quite interested and honored. I can come right now in fact. You've just saved me one dog day afternoon."

"Well, you've saved me one as well, Miss Orville. How long will you be?"

"Say, about forty minutes. I'll start off right now."

46

"I'll be ready."

Florence wasted no time in preparing herself, then venturing outside the Villa to the Civic, in which she started towards Bianca's house. She was nearly a mile out before she realized something with a start. "You damned Florence fool," she snapped. "Forgot to ask her for directions!"

And yet something seemed for some reason to be telling her just where to make a turn, how far---even how fast to go. Not a matter of remembering, or even of some of the figures in her mind. Just some kind of gut feeling---a sixth sense or instinct. "Now what's making me know where and when to turn?" she inquired of her bewildered self. "Could it be the beginning stages of deterioration or regression? Am I becoming…an…*animal?*" She continued on and forward until coming to a stop thirty-nine minutes from the start of her trip---in front of Bianca's house.

"Well, whatever it was," she mused, "it's certainly gotten me to my destination on time. Still, better learn my lesson to confirm directions next time." Then she exited the Civic and approached the house.

Sixteen

"Ah, Miss Orville," Bianca smiled upon opening the front door. "I'm happy to see you've made it here."

Florence sensed a mild yet considerable tension within her despite her best efforts to put on a gracious face, but decided not to mention it for now as she suspected she would learn its true source soon enough (indeed, she had a feeling she would learn more than she might have wanted). *That instinct in me again!* She frowned to herself.

"Well, I'm happy to be invited here," she replied, trying to humor the air a little. "Yesterday you visit my lair, today I visit yours. How acquaintive!"

"Certainly ironic," Bianca said, not really following Florence's lead. "A shame I haven't any food to offer, but---"

(*"That's not really why you've invited me here,"* Florence thought.)

"---it's a little more important than that," Bianca continued, suddenly grasping Florence's hand. "Let's...go down to the basement---it's a temporary museum of sorts for Breed at the moment."

Before Florence could reply, Bianca was already leading her along some path through the main rooms. The quickness of her steps as she moved confirmed Florence's suspicions about something being amiss. Still, Florence dared not ask---something was telling her this was not quite the time to inquire and that there was nothing Breed had to fear from this woman---yet suddenly she was not so sure about Bianca herself.

Taking advantage of the "tour" Bianca was giving her, she glanced at the rooms she was being rushed through. There was a large and spacious stairway leading upstairs from the foyer ("Presumably to the main bedrooms," she thought). The furnishings all appeared to be well kept, and the décor had a sort of old-world ornateness about each room. She noted pictures of men and women on the walls of the living room---seemingly Victorian in style (especially with those picture frames one found mostly in museums of fine art these days), though resembling Bianca (indeed, a couple were clearly of Bianca as a younger woman) as a family resemblance would, only with sterner countenances than Bianca herself would seem capable of displaying towards anyone, least of all Breed.

The dining room had a large oak table with seating arranged in family-style (*"Obviously,"* Florence observed, "not in use to full capacity these days."), and on one wall was a large mirror with similar frames to the pictures. A quick glance into the kitchen revealed a gas stove and large refrigerator, and another, smaller dining area just beyond it.

Bianca stopped at a door just off the kitchen, pulled a set of keys out of a pocket, and unlocked it, revealing a stairway going downward. "This way, Miss Orville," she said seriously to Florence as she turned on a light. The light was insistent but accommodating. Florence did not sense any deception or danger in it, so she let Bianca lead her downstairs.

"And here we are," Bianca said once Florence had joined her at the bottom of the stairs. Looking around her, Florence realized the room had some drawn, sometimes painted, and a few pasted collages, all of artwork, posted on the walls. And all of them had been done by Breed. But what started Florence most was the ominous graphicness of some of them. Certainly some of this was more violent than any that she had seen of Breed's work of her.

"…uh, Mrs. San Cortez," she inquired, I can tell all this is Breed's…is anything wrong…or…"

"No, no," Bianca said as though she might have added *not yet*, "at least not with his relationship with me, or even of his art. He probably couldn't have picked a better outlet for his demons than this."

"I note that some of those demons use white picket fences," Florence said, "and nuclear plants with nuclear families inside. Not very subtle about families, I see."

"And that's the key," Bianca sighed. "I didn't say anything before, because I knew he was afraid of what you'd think of him, but after that call…I just thought I'd better prepare myself. You see, Miss Orville, Breed was a product of incest."

"Incest?"

"His father is also his grandfather and his mother is also his sister."

Florence stood jarred, not by this revelation, but rather at her own lack of reaction to it; it was as though she had sensed it all along and had even deduced it some time ago. "Not a happy home life that could have been," was all the reply she could think of.

"What situation like that could be?" Bianca replied bitterly. "A hateful one. She hated Breed for his reminding her of the terrible ordeal of being raped by her own father, who hated Breed because he was not the *Strong God-fearing MAN* he was supposed to be. And *his* wife hated Breed because he reminded her of her own inability to have anymore children after her daughter was born---and Breed was a symbol used by her husband to rub her nose in it. He had even named him Breed as a reminder of the golden rule she had violated as a wife and mother.

"He had been kicked out of the home at thirteen, and found himself stuck in foster care and orphanages, where the circumstances of his birth had been used as a club to hit him with, even by the staff and house parents. He had been involved with something at his last board-and-care---rather violent and which could have resulted in his instigator's death after a particularly rough taunting. But his art saved him in a way at most other times---letting himself out through it enabled him to release his demons enough to avoid anymore incidents. But he's so fragile in many ways, Miss Orville...and he's so still in need of someone to love and respect him."

This was what would take its time to sink in to Florence's soul. Her own childhood situation had been terrible, but Breed's had been worse still. And unlike her, Breed had had no mentors to free him or otherwise offset the home torments until very late---when his psyche had already been scarred perhaps for life. Something told her that this was what those instincts were telling her was the truth of her visit here. But there were still some unanswered questions, and now was the time to ask them.

"I've been doing this for some time now," Bianca went on, "and don't get me wrong; I've no regrets about it and would do it for life. He is a very worthy person."

"Yes," Florence agreed. "*But*."

"But...?" This startled Bianca, as Florence had intended.

"You said something about a call."

"Yes," Bianca murmured resignedly, seeing there was no way out. "From my own family. Miss Orville, I'm from a very prominent family---I mean *very* prominent---and very powerful. Some of us have...diplomatic connections..."

"And diplomatic immunity?" Florence asked, even though she could already guess what Bianca was getting at.

"True, though I'm not at liberty to elaborate on *that*."

Florence sensed that it would not be wise to press Bianca on that part of the matter. "But how does it affect Breed?" she did inquire.

"In that they never much approved of my taking in boarders or artists after my husband's death, but they did *tolerate* it---until they learned of Breed."

Florence was developing an ominous hunch about this, but kept it to herself for the time being. "And were all the others---"

"*Caucasian men, Miss Orville*," Bianca interrupted as much in desperation as impatience. "*Caucasian---plus a couple of Asians and maybe an Arab or Latino*."

That was all Florence needed to know.

"That call I got," Bianca continued, "was from---relatives. And I won't give you details, but it was not very friendly *at all*. Right after they hung up, you called me, and that's why I've just told you all of this. Breed respects---even idolizes you enough that I must now request that should the worst happen---" She paused, as if trying to suppress a sob. "---that you'll help him survive and protect him."

"Oh my goodness," Florence gasped, reeling at the gravity of all this despite herself. "That is an unusual request..." ("...and I'm...not sure if I'm at all qualified..." she continued in her head.)

Bianca was aware that this was a life decision she was asking of Florence. "I realize, Miss Orville, how strange and sudden my request must be," she said. "You need not answer right now."

Florence tried to conceal her obvious relief at that. "Mrs. San Cortez, you do know I'd be willing to do what I can for Breed---"

"I didn't think otherwise, Miss Orville," Bianca replied. "My apologies for imposing so abruptly, but you realize how urgent this has become."

"I do," Florence replied. *All too well.*

Seventeen

And although Florence had meant that as strongly as then, this required some thinking over, and not just in her home. So it was that she found herself at the lookout point, her first trip there in a while, where she stood, leaning on the side of her car, looking on at the panorama of the city below (though technically she was still within the city limits).

"And somewhere within this vast city of many a tale," she mused to herself, "one Breed Hamilton is displaying his talents, a story creating many pictorial stories from within, borne of some vivid stories of his own. All of us are that way, really---some of us are more blatant and honest about it."

Staring at the lights flickering like small dots in the distant view, she imagined one such light (it didn't really matter from where) rising up from the grounds of the city and enlarging as it rose up, up, upwards until it was at a height parallel with her line of sight, and life-size. At this point it opened up as though it were a portal into a different location. Within the location she could picture Breed working at his makeshift easel, doing drawing upon drawing of warmly appreciative passersby and handing some of the works away. "All those stories and art he must be making folks happy by," she observed. "And they seem genuinely happy and moved too. Nobody more so than yourself, huh, Breed? Would that I could be so moved by things again. But alas…" She did not continue, but let herself look in longing at this scene. Hallucinations again? Maybe. But she'd let herself take it all in. How long? She never truly found out, but it didn't matter. What did was that Breed was fulfilling himself and his potential despite all that had tried to hold back and even destroy him and---she had to say it this way---doing a damned good job of it!

"But *for how long?*" a thought pattern cut in, causing her to curse.

Something made her whirl about, catching a flashlight's glare in her face. Involuntarily, she gasped and threw her hands over her eyes to shield them.

"Sorry, miss," the policeman with the flashlight said, lowering it slightly. "We were just curious."

"About *what?*" she said, suppressing a hiss.

"About if you realize how dark it already is."

Regaining her senses, she noted that it was quite late and that the moon was out. But inwardly she was breathing fire---*how dare you interrupt my wonderful enjoyment of Breed Hamilton---dream-self or not!* At a more day-ridden time and with better preparation and stamina she might have been tempted to call these pimply-faced beach boys (there were two of them; one was behind the wheel of their car, parked almost directly behind hers) barely half her age, on their pampered and privileged impunity. But now was not such a time, lucky for *them*.

"Oh...how careless of me," she said in mock-coquettishness, "being so enhanced by the view...why, I forgot the time!"

"Well, just be careful next time," the officer at the wheel lectured from the car's window.

"Yeah!" the first one added. "Who knows what mugger or other predator could be lurking!" And with pride, he went back inside the squad car, which brusquely turned and sped away.

"Or *police officer*," Florence said defiantly as she watched it depart. After several minutes in which she waited for the car to fade from sight, and deliberately waiting a bit longer after that, she stepped in her own car and, gunning it into reverse, backed into the road, jerked into forward and rocketed off for her home.

By the time she had arrived there she had spent her resentment over being lectured to and was in a reasonably relaxed mood as she stepped out of the car. As she had more or less expected out of resignation, Dashiki Drab was there, stern of eye.

"*Lying traitors deserter of Nubian pride!*" he bellowed. "*You have long worked in complicity with the Devil of the Domination to keep your own aspiring people down and docile and, like the boy Kamil-Abdul whose identity you stole from him for the slave name of Dion Hapless and whom you have martyred in the name of the white man---*"

"Unfortunately too true," Florence replied gently as she nonchalantly passed him to approach her front door.

Her placidity somehow seemed to aggravate him. *"COME BACK HERE FLORENCE ORVILLE!"* he thundered. *"YOU CANNOT JUST WALK BY AFTER YOUR CONFESSION TO SEDITIOUS TREASON OF THE AFRIKAN DIASPORA---"*

"Sure I can," she smirked as she entered her house and clicked the door shut behind her.

"Oh that was so cruel," she said to herself once inside before sighing. "But to such as him, I committed seditious treason simply by being born. Perhaps he is right to call me a traitor. But give him the slightest satisfaction of that knowledge? Especially just because I was born? *Never!*" And she strode up the stairway to her room, in which she retired for the evening in triumph.

Eighteen

"What's this...?" Florence asked herself as she was wandering in the oak's branches. "I don't recall seeing this extremity before..." It was a branch, or rather, a long, unusually thick branch with an equally unusually thick group of its own branches, almost a sort of steep, rocky trail.

"Well," she smiled, "that path's most tempting, and I've nothing better to do today." Though it was somewhere in an unusually empty night, she could see her way about and started to make her way along the path.

"Could this be my very own yellow brick road?" she mused as she crept, pushed, pulled and heaved herself through the foliage that was just packed, dense and challenging enough to pique her interest in conquering it. "Or the rainbow I'm somewhere over. Perhaps this is some sort of overground rabbit hole---"

At that moment the branch her foot was pressing on broke suddenly, causing her to gasp involuntarily; but for her instinctual reflexes in increasing her grip with her hands and arms she might have fallen off. For an instant she dangled above the ground, legs swinging, but was able to wrap one, then both of them around the branches, and heave herself to a safe position.

"Lucky I've not lost too much of my supple physicality!" she laughed in relief. "That was awfully close---but at least I kept both shoes on." Then she continued on her way.

After a while she noted that the branches were branching out, and most were entering into windows, seemingly those of various homes. "Wonder of wonderment," she thought. "Is this some sort of natural parkway I'm on? Or some odd, quaint town? I hope---for their sake---I'm not on one of those private roads in some gated community...but then I don't recall coming across a gate much less---"

And then she saw one particular window.

"*That's Mrs. San Cortez's window!*" she gasped. "Funny---I don't recall any extended branch creeping into her house when I was there before, and yet this looks so familiar...might as well stop by and visit, though."

So she pushed and shoved and squeezed herself to and then through the ("*Naturally!*" she could not help saying in sarcasm) open window and found herself standing in what was obviously Bianca's bedroom.

"And quite a pantry of a bedroom it is," she observed. "Very classy woman, that Bianca. But she's obviously not in here; maybe she's downstairs."

Walking out of the bedroom and making her way to the house's central area, she found herself looking down upon a most unusually-looking rotunda from which every room in the house could be seen ("Now *what* kind if architect could come up with *that!*" Florence joshed). Peppered through some of the rooms were a few of Breed's portraits and those of other artists that Florence could not immediately recognize; in one of the lower rooms she spotted Breed himself, happily asleep, which warmed her immensely for some reason (*Oh wonderful! Getting maternal are you--- occupational hazard of my old age perhaps?*). In the main living room (the most central of the views), she found---

"*Dona Bianca!*" she called out in delight. Bianca was seated wistfully in an easy chair, a tranquil expression on her face.

"Bianca!" Florence called out again. "It's me, Florence Orville!" But Bianca took no apparent notice.

"How peculiar," Florence noted. "I called her twice, virtually to her face…and no answer. Must be asleep though her eyes seem to be open. Maybe I'd best---"

The thunder of doors being kicked in by heavy boots brought a violent end to her train of thought, whirling her to the view of the front foyer, where a number of men, two in full suits with ties, most in some type of paramilitary uniform, had just burst in, and from which she could hear furious orders being barked as the men scattered about.

She somehow knew that this was a very bad sign. *"Trouble!"* she nearly screamed just before Bianca's earlier request to her echoed in her head--- *"---you'll help him survive and protect him?"*

"Well, they're not here *yet!"* she vowed without considering how she was making all these deductions, or how she was going to fend these intruders off by herself. "And I'll make damned sure they'll be sorry they so much as *thought* about entering this abode!" And she darted into a lightning sprint toward the front foyer.

But just as she was whirling herself to face the intruders, something caught her by the back of the neck and she had barely enough time to let out a reflexive squeal before she was yanked into a closet, after which the door was slammed shut behind her.

"Let me go, damn you!" Florence snapped and struggled wildly, but the closet's combined space and her abductor's large size and strength combined to subdue her.

"No you don't, little girl," a familiar voice grinned at her. "You ain't stopping nobody's past handiwork." Just then he pressed something and Florence felt the closet going upwards, as if it was an elevator. "But I was on the top floor!" she thought to herself in disbelief.

Then the abductor clicked on the light and Florence could see her captor---the man in the white suit.

"Father," she said coldly.

Nineteen

The closet door opened and Florence was shoved out of the small enclosure onto the ground outside. Looking about her, she surveyed that she was somehow in a grotto of sorts, quite unlike any that she had ever been to; rather, this seemed almost like an area similar to being at or near the summit of one of the Himalayas, though curiously with no sign of snow or glaciers. She noted the man was looking at her with snide bemusement.

"Think it's all funny don't you?" she hissed at him. "I already know you're dead."

"Oh dear, so I am," he replied. "But in a sense…especially yours, little daughter…I'm just as alive as I once was. But let me show you as I am in many ways---I'll show you the me you know and love."

Florence stiffened herself as if suspecting he was about to jump her, but instead he pulled at himself until his wide-brimmed hat was off, then his white bowtie and suit, so was his moustache and hair and finally his skin itself, revealing as he enlarged to gigantic proportions, a white-bearded man, beard only slightly darker and shorter than that of a bizarrely-bloated yet much more powerfully-muscled Santa Claus, and the laugh that burst forward was every bit as throaty, albeit with a sinister edge to it. He gazed down at Florence, whose glare was one of awe and defiance.

"Know who I am!" he thundered. "Many have I been called, little Florence, but you can call me MASTER ZEUS!"

"Master Zeus," she said disparagingly as though she had known exactly what she was up against and was not at all impressed by it.

"Yes, MASTER ZEUS!" he bellowed in fury, wounded by her disinterest. "The master of those of all he sees and encounters! Of the Red one the Black one the Yellow one the Brown one and even the White ones---and ESPECIALLY through the women to whom I have long bestowed my passion my greatness of seed upon through---out the eternities! Siring many and diluting all the in---ferior mongrel years in the mingling of their blood into mine and indoctrinating the offspring so as to destroy all knowledge of their inferior cultures from their minds! I have had born of all the wo---men the Cherry, the Chocolate the Lemon the Caramel and yes, even the Vanilla ones---and YOU are one of mine!"

"Oh swell," Florence deadpanned, "I'm the daughter of Yertle the Turtle."

"You---IM---PUDENT   BASTARD!" Master Zeus roared, thunder and lightning erupting around him in his fit of pique. "You DARE mock the Master---YOUR MASTER AND LORD???!!!" He paused as if to calm himself, as the thunder and lightning ceased.

"Well, you're the one who sired this bastard," Florence said, not having lost an ounce of her defiance and definitely not having any of his outrage. "And since I'm likely to be destroyed anyway, I might as well get my jabs in."

But instead of going for her, Master Zeus reached behind a mountain outcrop and pulled up a seemingly battered knight's helmet. "You are quite right in the circumstances of my part in your creation," he said jovially. "But let you rest as---

sured that what I have crea---ted I can also des---
TROY!" After putting the helmet on his head, he
gestured upwards, and a bolt of lightning shot from
his hand and became a sword. "A pre---tense of
Saint George should do quite nice---ly to finish you
off, foolish bastard Florence. HO-HO!!"

It was at this point that Florence noted that
she too was beginning to enlarge as if to meet
Master Zeus on equal terms. Yet this
transformation was different, for as her clothes were
stretching then splitting and tearing to shreds, and
her feet were deforming and finally bursting out of
her shoes ("This time my shoes didn't survive," she
joshed), she noted her skin was not only developing
reptilian scales and thickening to armor-like
resiliency but was also taking on a dark greenish
tint, her body was becoming more massive, her
fingernails and toenails had shape-shifted into
talons, and that her nostrils were emitting puffs of
flaming smoke.

"Oh my," she thought. "This is most
unusual, my nose spewing up smoke and my body
sprouting like this. I look much like I normally do,
except I'm big as a skyscraper, scaly, green and
now nude to boot. Well, least I seem to have kept
my hair. So this is Miss Dragonheel---only I'm in
bare heels now. Could this be perm---"

Here musing ended with a cry (or roar?)
from her, more from surprise than pain, as the flat
of Master Zeus' blade slapped upon her cheek.

"Silly she-dragon!" he blared in jest. "Now
is hardly the time to reason why---yours is but to
meet your des---tiny! Your FATE! You can---not
fight the role!"

"Oh shut up!" she growled, and lunged to
slap him back. But she had misjudged her leap,

having neglected to reckon with or take into account her greater size, mass, and muscle distribution, or her heavier, taloned hand with which she had intended to strike him. She impacted with the earth clumsily, as if she had tripped over her larger feet. Something---another hunch?---warned her to roll over just in time to avoid skewerment by Master Zeus' thunderous blade as she cursed herself for her new-found clumsiness.

"O THE FLESH AND SPIRIT ARE MIGHTY BUT THE EXPE---RIENCE AND COORDINATION ARE NOT!" Master Zeus jeered. "AND YOUR DEFIANCE IS GREATEST OF ALL FOR YOU STILL DO NOT ACCEPT WHO YOU ARE!" He charged at her.

"Damn him for being so right!" Florence seethed to herself as she kicked back his assault.

"BUT I AM TRIED OF THESE GAMES!" he went on. "LET ME JUST PUT YOU AWAY, FOOLISH FLO---RENCE, WHERE YOU WILL SUFFOCATE AND PUT A MOST DE---SERVED END TO YOUR ARROGANT WIND!"

He waved his arms up and the entire world seemed to shake around Florence as though she were at the epicenter of a gigantic earthquake. Before she could get her bearings a chasm violently opened beneath her feet and she plunged into it.

"No!" she shrieked as the earth crashed about her, then smashed itself shut, compressing her within it.

Twenty

"Now this is most uncomfortable," Florence thought, for she could not easily speak underneath how many tons of rock and earth she was sandwiched within and fighting off and grasping against all at once. "Me, Florence Susan Orville, being pancaked and chewed up by the earth itself. The whole world's *really* against me tonight! I suppose I'd best try to get out of this, for the air won't last much longer---*uhnn!*---but it's so hard trying to hold my own against the world itself---*ohn!*---this form not helping matters much; been more the liability than the---*hmmp!*---asset, so clumsy I've been. *Ha!* Such levity I display---*oomph!*---in what's certainly my last moments of human existence---"

Something came to her like a shot. "*Human existence!* Some human *I* turned out to be...more dragon now than---" She stopped again. Then she remembered one of Master Zeus' phrases: "*AND YOUR DE---FIANCE IS GREATEST OF ALL FOR---*"

"---*you---still---do---not---accept---who---you---are!*" she thought. "Maybe *that's it! Perhaps*---if I surrender---let Miss Dragonheel rise within me---rise to all her glory..." She need not have continued, for she was already numbing herself into the cauldron that housed that terrible nature of hers---the nature that had smote many a cocky dream and shattered those of more sensitive souls such as Dion Justice's.

Somehow she found herself observing the violence of her physical resistance to the earth's struggle to contain her, her clawing, twisting, kicking---the intensity of the fire spewing from nose and mouth, the battle to precipitate an explosive crescendo---

And it did.

The force of the release that freed her sent Master Zeus reeling in astonishment for the instant between his would-be captive's breakout of her intended entombment and her primal lunge at him. Florence thought he had attempted to boast about how she could not have possibly overcome the Master's plans for her and even tried to wield his thunder-sword, but she was on him before he could react.

The impact of the initial lunge sent Master Zeus propelling into a stone reef; surprised and infuriated, he attempted to regain his equilibrium and reassert his mastery but his former captive struck him down. Lightning-swift, he started to rise but Miss Dragonheel caught him as he reached his full height with a blast of fire-breath, then, using one clawed hand, raked at the stunned Master. Then, without even thinking to see if she had drawn blood, she threw herself on him and proceeded to tear, batter and kick her former tormentor for what seemed to be a length of time that could only be guessed at.

Only the choked sob of a child caused she who was Miss Dragonheel to pause. Florence, upon this opportunity, seized control of herself back from Miss Dragonheel and looked around her. The once-imposing form of Master Zeus was in shredded pieces, like a rag doll torn asunder. Among the pieces sat a young, nude blond boy of kindergarten age pleading upward to the still gigantic and dragon-like form of Florence.

"*NoMommynodDaddynononomoreI'llbego odI'llbegoodnomorepleasenomore---*"

"No more *WHAT!!!*" screamed Florence, still steeped in rage and anguish. "You act like you're the god of gods almighty, rape the women and spurn the bastards who result from your antics and torment and bully and ride all about them and turn them into the very things you accuse them of being. Look at me---*LOOK AT ME!* You made me into this demon I am! I may be too late for me BUT I'LL BE DAMNED IF I'LL LET YOU PERVERT AND DISTORT ANY MORE PEOPLE! So go ahead and hide in your brat form---" She lifted her foot and held it over the child as though to crush him with it. "---*I'LL DESTROY YOU IN ANY DAMN FORM YOU WANT!!!*"

"*NOOOOOOOOOOOOOOOOOOOO!!!!!*" the boy screamed as Florence lowered her foot.

"No, Florence...please don't."

The soft, matronly voice caused Florence to hesitate. She looked about her and saw some sort of gentle ebony smoke emitting from the eyes, nose and mouth of the remains of Master Zeus' head. The smoke coalesced into a form of sorts a few feet from the head's brow before refining itself into the form of an elegant black woman in royal African garb.

"*Mother---?*" Florence gasped in disbelief.

And yet it was not the mother as Florence remembered her, but the mother as she might have been had she been allowed to discover and nurture her potential, had her ancestors not been stolen from the homeland, sold into slavery or endured all that her people had had to suffer, and if the mother herself had never had to join forces with a nationalist, been raped by a racist or been shamed by the husband thereafter. This was the mother as she might have been, and who now approached the frightened child she had just stopped Florence from crushing under her foot.

"Is it you...Mother?" Florence asked in a whisper.

"Yes and no, my daughter. You see me as I should have been---for myself and for you."

"And what am *I?*" she pleaded. "Look at me---*look what he did to me!*"

"He and I and my husband all," the Mother said, "and most essentially, your nature. You are who you are, child. You have me within you, the product of Nubian queens and kings, you have him---" She picked up the boy and held him close to her bosom. "---not the 'Master Zeus' which you see torn to shreds, but he who is the product of great peoples too, hard as it is for you to see right now. And you are Miss Dragonheel, a force capable of terror, or, should you accept and hone her well, a force of greatness. Utilize your elements, my Florence...accept them as they are indelibly you."

"But he raped you and---"

"That is immutable, and no fault of yours," the Mother said, "nor is my reaction to it. All three of us did you terrible wrongs, but that burden should not be borne by you. Learn from all your parts and use them as gifts, for even now you are sorely needed."

Florence gasped, for she now remembered what had started this adventure. *"Breed! Dona Bianca!* I---I forgot about them!"

She turned and bolted off, towards a cliff, jumping over its edge into the air, and, as if knowing how to do so all along, glided herself until she was over the neighborhood of Bianca's house, then alighted herself carefully, for she was now many stories high and did not wish to risk stepping on something, and looked into the house.

But the yards around it were cluttered askew with what she realized to her horror were the remains of Breed's pictures. There was some furniture among the mess as well, and both Breed and Bianca were gone.

"No---*no*," she cried in desperation, "oh my god---*no! I'm too late…I…I took too long---with Master Zeus---I'm too late---TOO LATE!*" Covering her face with her hands, she began to weep inconsolably, and, though she barely noticed it in her grief, she began to shrink reasonably until she had finally reverted to her normal size and appearance, only vaguely noting the cold night air caressing her naked form. *"Oh, Breed---oh Bianca…forgive me for failing you…! I'm sorry--- I'm so sorry---!"*

"It is not your fault," she heard the Mother's voice say. "What you saw earlier had already happened; that was why Dona Bianca did not respond when you tried to greet her earlier. You could not have stopped anything even had you not been abducted, it had already happened. But you can still be of aid…remember what I said…you are still sorely needed…"

But Florence could only repeat, "I'm sorry---I'm sorry---!"

She woke up with a start from her bed. Looking frantically around her, she realized she had just had "one hell of a dream!" as she spoke aloud.

Putting her hand to her face, she realized it was quite wet. "And a most passionate one too!" Then, as though not quite believing it had all been a dream, she examined her body, her limbs, fingers and toes, all of which were very much her normal human ones, and after reassuring herself that she was no dragon (at least physically), shifted herself to a seated position, arms wrapped around her knees.

"Well," she mused to herself, "that dragon-form of mine would not have easily fit in this house anyway; perhaps it's just as well I didn't really become that, though there *was* something exhilarating...even *risqué*...about it. But at least it means that Breed and Dona Bianca are safe in bed---though presumably not the same bed."

She sat up on her own bed for the remainder of the night and was unable to resume sleep until the dawn began to break through.

Twenty-One

Somehow the ringing of her phone snapped Florence to attention, as if her instincts knew of its urgency. It seemed to her that the rings were much louder than usual, but assured to her that it was simply that she had been in a part-awake, part asleep state. Pulling herself to the edge of her bed, she reached the phone and picked up the receiver.

"Hello---?"

"Oh thank goodness...oh, Florence---oh, god---*god-d-d-d!*"

"Breed?"

"Yes---*yes!*"

Something was very wrong, she could tell. *Terribly* wrong.

"Breed, what is it? What's the matter?"

"Everything, Florence---*everything!*" His voice was broken, the second "everything" was almost screamed out. From what she could hear, Florence knew he would not be able to give details in such an anguished state. What could have happened? And what of Bianca? Could something have happened to her (and was it why Breed apparently had not turned to her first)? Alas, these inquiries would have to wait. All but one crucial one.

"Breed, where are you?" *Keep yourself composed, woman.*

"The...the hospital..."

"Which one?"

"Fair...Fairmount...the psychiatric unit."

"Hang on, Breed," Florence replied. "I'm going to start out there now. Give me about--- twenty to twenty-five minutes. And try to pull yourself together."

"I'll---I'll try," Breed choked. "But---but it's so hard---!"

"I know, dear," she said with genuine sympathy. "Just hang on 'till I can get there."

"O---okay."

Upon hanging up, she fitted herself into the nearest of clothing she could find with a speed that might have rivaled any in her dream-adventure of the night before. But that was out of her mind at the moment, as was (*"For once!"* she would exclaim with realization about midway to the hospital) her appearance and grooming (though even then she didn't really look bad by any standard, even in a rush job of dressing). As soon as she had thrown together some kind of attire, she was out the door and into her car, and by the following minute was on her way.

Upon entering the hospital parking lot, she spotted Breed slumped on a bench beside its entrance. It was a position so unlike him that it took her longer than she had expected to recognize him. It hurt her deeply to see him like that, as if his entire world had ended by extreme violence. As soon as she found an empty parking space, she shot into it, stopped the car and rushed out to meet him. She could tell that he had not apparently noticed her.

"Breed!" she called out as she reached him. He looked up at her and she caught a look at his horribly tear-stained face. "Are you all right? You sounded so frantic."

"All right---?" he near-whispered. "I'm...not so sure I'll ever be---*again*..." He broke off, as though about to weep again. Crouching down to be eye-to-eye with him, she wrapped her arms around him in consolation.

"What of your art?" she asked without really thinking about it. "It's helped you before."

"It's gone---all...gone. Bianca's...gone too."

"You mean she's in---" she asked, thinking for an instant that she was dead.

"No---no---*no*," he cried as if ready to explode. "She's---just gone! Not dead...just...gone..." His anguish was such that it was all that Florence could do to keep her own emotions in check.

"Calm down, Breed," she murmured with extreme delicacy, "calm down. I'm here now. Listen, let's head home---"

"I can't go home---any more---" he said gravely.

"I mean my home," she corrected herself. "Once we're there we can discuss this further and I can offer you something; I didn't bring anything to eat or drink. And some fool won't likely see this and sic the police on us there."

That seemed to make him slightly more composed. "No---no---no more police...those bastards. Can we go---"

"As soon as you wish."

"*Now*...please," he said, struggling to rise. She offered her support and he pulled himself up, as if crippled. She held her arms about his upper body and he leaned upon her. Locked in this co-supportive clasp, they trudged to the Civic, Florence gently leading the way.

Nothing was said during the drive back. Breed sat slumped in the passenger's seat as if asleep. Florence dared not say anything, even though she had volumes to inquire. But she did not want to risk setting off anything in Breed during the trip; the Italianate Villa would be a much more suitable venue for seeking answers.

But not before Breed had been settled down and helped to some refreshments, which Florence promptly saw to once they were safely inside. Once she had been able to unwind herself, she realized, as she watched him down each refreshment gingerly, the hard fact of his contradiction---as large and formidable as he looked, that was how delicate, even fragile---he seemed to be. Were the situation less volatile it might have struck her as rather funny as to how long it had taken her to realize that. Instead she could only utter a sad sigh to herself.

Somebody had to stay on an even keel here, "---and it looks like I've been elected," she surmised.

Not long after she somehow discovered that now was the time to make her move. *Go easy---this time, Orville. This is no time for your energy to display itself improperly.*

"Breed...?"

He looked up at her with an expression that assured her that he was now composed enough to at least try to provide details.

"What happened, dear? Where is Bianca...is she...?"

"I...wish I knew...for sure," he said, calm but still fighting his emotions. "I---I---don't even know where to begin---!" he looked for a time as though he was about to burst. Instinctively, Florence reached out and touched his hand with hers, which seemed to steady him as though her touch anchored him to firmer ground.

"Just start at the top," she reassured him.

"I...guess I'll have to," he said with soft intensity.

Twenty-Two

Breed was straddling the borders between sleep and awareness of things, as though he were awake, somewhere in dreamland or about to depart or in the middle of it---he couldn't remember what now---when a thundering explosion occurred near him.

"There he is!"

"Get him out of that bed!"

"Up, you boy! MOVE!"

It happened so fast, the door being kicked open, the belongings in the room being upset or ripped from the walls, in a crescendo of jumbled noises, and finally, his form yanked out of the bed, hurled between men and shouted at to his face, was pulled roughly to the exposed doorway and shoved in violent directions.

Breed desperately closed his eyes. But the tumult continued.

A slap across his face jerked his eyes open. "You---*get out! GET HIM OUT OF HERE!*"

"What---what's going---"

"*SHUTUPBOY!*" Another shove, this time broken by the grabbing of both arms that nearly yanked them out of their sockets. More shoves, a few kicks along the way. He could hear Bianca's voice along with another's.

"*Leave him alone! He's not done anything to deserve this---leave him alone---leave him be!*"

"*You have no right to speak woman you who have transgressed as you have we have been lenient up to now but NO MORE...*"

He got a glimpse of some other of them tearing the portraits off the walls as though they were strips of old wallpaper. "What are you doing no don't do that that's---"

"*SILENCE!*" And a sledge hammering kick to the stomach.

Upon the feel of a minor breeze (which indicated that he was now outside), he felt himself propelled none too gently onto the cement driveway, where from his prone and stunned position he could see several pairs of combat boots around him ready to strike at the most minute of opportunities; from the corner of his eye he saw various papers---*his* papers of their works (or what remained of them) being carelessly tossed in numerous directions with the background of *"What's the use of these worthless things anyway this one thought he's Picasso or something forget it we're done here now no please why do you do this because you have gone too far have you forgotten your place foolish woman now off with you what about him leave him to the vultures besides the authorities will be here soon they'll know what to do with all this refuse."* And the boots departed with them (though not before a few of them tred deliberately on him). A few slammed doors, at least two sets of screeching tires, and the departing roar of engines.

Breed's blinking was desperate. *Wake up man, wake up!*

He stumbled desperately, heart pounding, breathing hard, running all over the place to gather the pieces of his artwork which the winds were using as pawns in this child's game of catch it if you can, catch them if you can. *No no, stop it wind, come on quit blowing like that I've got to catch them so I can then try to save Bianca why why why did they do such a terrible thing they took away Bianca the only one who cared just like everything I had's been taken away just like this wind's now taking away my work my life's work STOP IT WIND STOP IT I WANT BIANCA I WANT BIANNNNCAAAA!!! I need Bianca I need someone but NOBODY WANTS ME! Not my mama not my papa not any of the homes not the bastards who took Bianca AND NOT THIS GOD---DAMMED--- WIND!!* His choked sobs and wails echoed as he ran after and grasped as many of the papers as he could.

And then he saw them. One tall and fair, the other short and dark.

Both wore blue.

"There he is," growled the tall one. "Just like they told us."

"Um-hmmm," the short one replied, then turned. "All right, fun and games're over, bud. Your next event's taking place in the station. Drop those bundles."

"B-bundles...? They're---"

"He said *now!*" the tall one roared, smacking the bundle out of his hand. "Now I'm not in a good mood!"

"He's right you know," the short one shrugged. "You'd better cooperate...my partner's had a bad day."

"But my art...my art..."

They sprang upon him, and he felt himself being bent over, his head jerked nearly 360 degrees (or so it felt) by the whip cracking slap across his face, his hands shoved behind him to be cuffed, and, then himself being roughly dragged between them to the squad car, in which the tall one flung him inside.

"C'mon," he barked to his partner. "Let's take this garbage to the station."

"Yeah," the small one replied, "but frankly, he needs a hospital more than a prison." Then he turned to Breed. "But since it's late, we'll have to house you in our cell for the night. Be a good boy and don't make anymore ruckus---my partner's real p.o.'ed tonight."

Breed recalled saying nothing (and feeling that) for the remainder of the night, not entering the station, not in the cell handcuffed to the rail of a cot, and not in the morning when he was indeed left off at the hospital---with neither regular clothes or any means of contacting anyone. Only a sympathetic nurse, apparently all too aware of the reputation of these particular officers, had found him some clothing and enabled him to use the desk phone to call Florence. He was not sure he could feel anything ever again---not after having lost everything.

Twenty-Three

Breed's eyes were closed in forlorn resignation. "That's...that's about it," he said in a crumpled whisper.

"You poor thing," Florence said consolingly, holding him close to her. "No wonder you're so broken up, after what you've gone through." Her façade was warm and gentle yet she burned inside with rage. Most of that rage was intended for the police and the men who had ripped apart his relationship with Bianca and torn his life's work to shreds, but a bit of it was meant for herself, for she knew that had something like this happened during her Miss Dragonheel days, she would not have been so compassionate---she would likely have been a tough-loving (but mostly tough) holy terror and probably shoved the poor thing back into action. No doubt many people today would say she'd have been admirable to do so. But not now and not Florence. Still, she knew that things would have to boil over as soon as possible once the full gravity of this terrible turn of events had settled in. Fortunately, she saw a minor way out.

"Listen, Breed," she said in as gently a maternal tone as she could muster. "I've got to go out for a bit, but I'll see if there's anything I can do to find out what happened to Bianca. I can't promise anything, but I intend to see what can be done. Meanwhile, you stay here as long as you wish; feel free to do as you wish, and if you get hunger or thirst pains, take whatever you need---but don't exert yourself too much, okay?"

He nodded, then slumped in quiet agony. She rubbed his back warmly and waited for him to rise in a sit-up position. As he did she let her hand leave his back for his face. "And those damned cops aren't going to bother you *any more*. Now I'd better go. And I'll be back." She got up and went to the door, paused, turned to Breed to smile at him, then stepped outside.

As she approached the Civic Dashiki Drab was there (sure enough).

"*For shame Florence Orville who now keeps young men who could be her sons! People are gonna talk about you---but at least---*" He snickered. "*---he's BLACK! Should I watch the pup for you!*" His tone was that of wicked, gleeful humor, but Florence was in no mood for it.

"You so much as think of bothering him I'll kill you," she warned him sternly.

"*Bother him---HA! It's you I'd rather 'bother!'*"

But Florence had already leaped into her car and sped off.

As soon as she was on her way Florence remembered a contact, one of several she had had while still at the Blanchstone Agency. One such contact had remained loyal to her, after nearly everyone else had cut her loose, and had even insisted she call on him whenever she needed to. "Well," she thought as she dialed her cell phone, "I guess this is such a time."

"Who is this?"

"It's me, Funston...Madame Dragonheel."

"About time you called. I wasn't kidding, or have you been straight and narrow all this time?"

"No such luck, Mister! Now seriously, I need your help on something. Last night, a friend of mine was abducted from her home, apparently by members of her family. Her name is Bianca San Cortez. Often with a *Dona* before it. A tall woman, about my age, with brown hair and eyes, I believe of Spanish-Argentine descent---"

"You know, Madame Dragonheel, you may be in luck. A couple of the guys on the grapevine say they're familiar with that name---the San Cortez name's pretty common in certain industries. Okay, I'll ask them and see what they can turn up."

"This is rather urgent, Funston."

"I realize that, Madame...in fact, someone said they overheard a plan from some big shot diplomats about some sort of kidnapping of a member of their own blood who want too far in their efforts. Don't worry, I'll get on it immediately."

"Thanks, Funston. Do all that you can."

"Always for you, Madame Dragonheel."

"Well," Florence went on after the cell phone conversation ended, "between the two of us, we just might learn what happened to Dona Bianca." And she promptly sped away towards Bianca's house.

Twenty-Four

When Florence arrived at Bianca's house she could not help but feel a cold eeriness about the site, "and not just from the chilly breeze," she mused to herself. The house that had seemed--- *been*---so full of life only a few days ago now looked terribly lost and abandoned. The door and main floor windows were covered over with fresh plywood, and those features and exteriors which had been regularly maintained looked as though maintenance had suddenly ceased, and scattered pieces of paper skipped all over the property.

"They sure managed to close up shop pretty quick," she observed as she inspected the property, "one can practically smell the remains of last night's dinner here...mingling with the early morning sawdust!" But her attempt at levity failed to ease her suspicions that the sudden shifting of the previous night involved forces far bigger than she or Breed could have realized.

Something brushed against and tickled her ankle, causing her to release a brisk, involuntary gasp. Looking down, she noted it was a badly crumpled sheet of paper. Picking it up to examine it, she realized that it was a portrait of Bianca and Breed together---one of Breed's portraits! "Oh, Breed! How sadly ironic," she sighed, and was about to let her tears flow a little when she stopped them in mid-transit. One of those hunches again.

She bent down again to examine the papers, picking them up as she passed them and silently reproaching herself for inadvertently stepping on some of them, which, given the way they had scattered all over the property, had been near-inevitable. She felt very much like one of those sleek women comic book detectives she read about on the sly as a young girl ("Thank goodness for cousin Donna and her comics aficionadolism," she chuckled to herself)---it dawned on her that her attire was not all that different from that of most of those lady shamuses. She liked that connection and irony.

Sure enough, the pieces were mostly of Breed's work. Most were torn asunder, a few almost to non-recognition, but she could tell they were his; only a few were mostly intact, and all were in crumpled states of disrepair to varying degrees. Still, she made sure to keep whatever she could find, perhaps---just *maybe*---Breed will be able to redo the work or salvage it in some way.

"Uh---*excuse* me---?"

Who dares! She wanted to hiss, but she kept her cool as she turned about to see an elderly man who had approached her from his own house, which was adjacent to Bianca's.

"You're looking for Mrs. San Cortez, madam?"

She had to catch herself a little, she had been caught off-guard. "Uh---yes. I'm an…associate of hers."

"Well, I'll tell you this…it was so darned bizarre, all that noise going on as if the place was under siege---or like one of those drug raids you hear about on the news. Never thought for a moment that *she* was into that, but maybe that boy who was with her last was; you know how *his* kind are into that stuff. Anyway, the police knocked on the door and told us to relax, everything was taken care of. Took forever for things to subside though."

"The boy---?" Florence suppressed an urge to blare about his reference to Breed as "that boy" and about his assumption of Breed's being into "that stuff."

"Oh he was---least I think it was him---he was carrying on about something or other---I recall now, he was screaming about art and about Mrs. San Cortez as though she was his mother. But eventually those cops came back and took him away from here. Couldn't sleep for the rest of the evening though. But soon as morning come up I looked out to see the place being boarded up as it is now. All I could get out of those folk was that Mrs. San Cortez wouldn't be back, they were real elusive about it all. I mean, maybe having that boy there and him being found out by the police was real embarrassing to her, but I never thought she'd just pack up and go so suddenly from it. Some folk sure touchy about their image I guess. Too bad too…she was a real classy woman."

Florence nodded in resigned agreement. *Breed was telling the truth, odd as it seems. And so, I fear, was poor Dona Bianca.*

"I see you're picking up some of the pieces," the man continued. "Though your attire don't seem proper for you doing that."

Oh it's not is it you nosy! Don't you realize whom you stand before? This is Miss Dragonheel, idol of poor Breed Hamilton whom you rudely dismiss as 'that boy!' and assume to be an illicit dope fiend. Too blind to be frightened are you!

"I got called to this assignment right after a more…elegant one," she replied. "Didn't even have time to change. But nobody said that she'd up and leave."

"Well, hope you find her, though frankly, looks to me like she won't be returning---period." Shaking his head, he turned and went back inside his house.

"You may be right," Florence whispered under her breath, and returned to picking up as many of the papers as she could handle.

But after a short time she noted there were no more significant papers to retrieve; those pieces that remained were too small or badly mangled to be of any use. She looked at the small heaps she had managed to assemble. "Well, Breed, hope this'll at least be of some salvage to you."

She returned to her car, where she piled the bundles as neatly as she could in the glove compartment, before driving away.

Twenty-Five

Florence's next stop was at a precinct of the police department. Rushing out of her parked car ("How much like the detective hot on a case, am I?" she wondered), she moved, determined toward the entrance and through the doors, where a desk sergeant stood behind the desk.

"May I be of assistance to you?"

"Yes, if you will," she replied, trying not to sound too desperate or too petulant. "I need to report about a missing person."

"Um---hmmm. May I have your name, please?"

"Florence Orville."

"And this missing person's name?"

"Her name is Bianca San Cortez."

"Bianca...San...Cortez---?" His young brow wrinkled as though he was supposed to be aware of something but turned out not to be. There was a mild silence. Florence realized that she had hit a most sensitive nerve.

"Uh, Miss Orville," he replied a little too professionally, "let me check this---thing out. Hey, Willie!" At his call an older officer came toward him and vice versa until they met halfway. Florence could only vaguely hear their brief conversation.

"What's up, Joe?"

"This lady's asking about..." His voice faded into a tense whisper, as did the other officer's, and Florence could no longer hear them. She did, in a subtle glance, continue to look on in case of gestures. The older officer's brusque nod signaled to her that something was up.

They returned to the desk at which she waited. It was the older one who spoke up. "Now let me get this straight, ma'am---you want to file a missing person's report on a Bianca San Cortez?"

"That I do."

"There's really no need to," the older officer replied. "We've received word that Mrs. San Cortez is quite all right; she's just flown back to her homeland."

"She *has?*" she pressed, feigning naïveté (but not very well, she believed).

"Yes," the younger officer said. "Some sort of diplomatic things requiring her---personal attendance. Not to worry, though, a lot of poor schmoes have tried this thing."

"Caught completely by surprise," the older one added. "Things came up so fast she had no time to notify anyone."

"So," Florence inquired, now feeling and feigning coquettishness, "the whole thing's been a case of Mrs. San Cortez's being called home to attend to some urgent matters, is that it?"

"*That's right!*" the officers beamed.

"Oh, then I guess I had this thing all wrong," she beamed back. "I'm glad---so glad to see that my friend's all right---I must be going, thank you so much." She turned and stepped towards the door, turning just long enough to add, "Sorry for being such trouble."

"No problem, ma'am," the younger one replied.

As she exited the precinct, Florence overheard one officer say "wasn't that that crazy Flo Orville?"

"I heard that," she thought to an imaginary version of the policemen. "You liars."

When she had driven several blocks from the police station, Florence pulled over to the nearest empty parking space and dialed her cell phone again.

"That you, Madame Dragonheel?"

"Yes, Funston. No luck on my front---what about you?"

"Mixed news, I'm afraid. I found out what you wanted, but it don't look like you'll be seeing any sign of Dona Bianca San Cortez anymore."

"She's...dead?"

"No, but in a way she might as well be. One of my grapevine's noted a good-sized crowd of about a dozen hurriedly rush onto this huge ocean liner sailing for Europe or somewhere. The one looking like Mrs. San Cortez didn't look too happy about it but that level of sadness means there ain't much to be done...you get my drift, Madame Dragonheel---?"

"Unfortunately, Funston, I do," she said sadly. "I'll send the money as soon as I can." *But how to explain this to a waiting Breed?*

Alas, even when she reached her house after deliberately taking the longest route she could think of, she was no closer to an answer to that question than when she had first thought it up. There was only one way to go about it, no matter how slowly she crept up the path to her own door. Dashiki Drab wasn't around; just like him to not be around when he really was needed for once.

Twenty-Six

Easing herself inside the house, Florence clicked the door shut and turned to find Breed seated on the couch---the same one she had left him at---clutching his head in violent agony as though he were considering trying to crumple his skull, and choked mutterings of *"why...why...why..."* broke from his throat. Muffled as a whisper yet thunderous in their impact. The sight of him took her aback; she barely had time to intercept a loud gasp from release. Did something happen while she was away? Or even Dashiki Drab? If *he* dared to---! No---let's first *find out why he's like this...*

"Breed?"

He made no move that could verify for her whether he heard her.

"Breed? It's me...Florence...I'm back...is...anything wrong?"

He could only grunt in agony as he motioned his finger beside and below him. It was then that she noted a crumpled piece of paper on the floor at his feet.

"Is this what you mean, dear?" she inquired as softly as possible.

"Yes…yes…*yes!*" he choked under his breath. She bent down to pick it up and began to straighten it up. It was a telegram.

"Read it and weep," he murmured in bitter sarcasm.

Florence did the former.

Breed, Breed, you poor foolish Breed. I took you in because I thought you to be someone with potential. Potential to be a great artist and a great man. Emphasis on the THOUGHT. I was wrong. I was also wrong to think that you were as worthy of my time and effort and compassion as the others I had taken in before. So where does that leave you, Breed Hamilton? A foolish, childish, pathetic fool who's looking for a breast to suckle and a mother figure to substitute for the one who had cast you out, and that, I fear, is all. A bizarre little Oedipus you are! Well, perhaps you will someday find that surrogate mother who will plant your sorry bloated carcass in your little crib, but I can rest assured that it will never be me; already the memory of your arms and hands around me in your puerile embraces makes me terribly giddy. You thought I loved you as I did the others---how foolish you are, kiddo! May we NEVER meet again.

With released contempt,
DONA Bianca San Cortez

A thoroughly stunned Florence let the telegram drop to her feet. She was at a complete loss over what to make of this; she was feeling quite giddy herself and a number of questions and possibilities whirled about in her mind. How could Bianca turn so coldly and cruelly against Breed like this? Had she really had hidden contempt for him all along---and for reasons thinly-veiled in their wording? If so, why had she not sensed it as she had sensed other hunches? Or were those really *her* words? It certainly seemed like a diction Bianca would have used, but could she have been forced to write this message or send it off? Could someone else (her captors) have written this and passed it off under her name? Or this scenario: maybe Bianca *did* write this note as a way of preventing Breed from entertaining any thought of trying to seek her out or of rescuing her---perhaps they had threatened to harm him? Or was it a means of pushing him to forget her and go on with his life and leave her to her fate? The multitude of potentialities overwhelmed her, in large part because she knew all too well that any, or some or even all of these possibilities had a chance of being absolutely true.

But one thing *was* certain: something had to be done for Breed who sat crumpled and defeated before her.

"Quite the vote of confidence, huh," he said, more a statement than an inquiry.

"I'm so sorry, Breed," she said with a sympathy still foreign to her yet sincere nonetheless. She hurt deeply for him; it was all she could do to keep from doing the second half of his earlier admonition.

"Why's that?" he said, not looking anywhere but straight down and ahead, bypassing her. "You've nothing to be sorry for---except maybe ever hearing of this bizarre little Oedipus named Breed Hamilton." He suddenly jerked his head upwards and uttered a loud, almost falsetto guffaw. "You'd think I'd be used to it by now; I've only been cast aside by nearly everyone I've ever known."

There was a subtle rise to his voice that unnerved Florence, for it seemed to be a signal that it was a violent calm right before something of cataclysmic magnitude. She could tell that something was about to explode; the best thing she could do at this point, however, was to ready herself---better to let it occur here where she might be able to somehow contain it with minimum risk to Breed than outside where most would *not* be so forbearing; the greatest risk here would be to herself. She steeled herself, praying that it would not prove to be beyond her capacities, and knowing innately that this was an upcoming baptism of fire for Miss Dragonheel.

"I---*should* be---used to this by now---!" Breed continued, his voice becoming more broken and higher-toned in places. "Why---why---why don't I enjoy this---I---I---*SHOULD* be enjoying this! I *should be cheerful!* Yes yes---*do it again HIT ME AGAIN! I LOVE ITILOVEITILOVEIT!*"

"Breed, don't do this to yourself," Florence pleaded. But she was all too aware that it was about to begin.

"Oh, no one around---?" he inquired as if nobody else was in the room. "Well then *I'LL DO IT MYSELF!*" Exploding to his full size, he swung his arms and with all kinds of frenzy began to batter himself with rapid-fire incessancy.

"*Breed, stop!*" Florence shrieked, now quite frightened for him, and rushed to him.

"But why not just the fists!" he cried. *"Let's try the ole throw against the wall!"* And he started to do just that, but Florence reached and intercepted him. Before she could secure herself, however, he shoved her away and completed his collision with the wall.

Undeterred, Florence rebounded and grasped Breed again, this time with a plan. Knowing she would not prevail in a standing battle, she swiftly forced Breed's leg from under him with her own, forcing him off-balance and causing him to topple, then embraced him fast as the momentum sent them to the floor, where the odds would be more even. Breed attempted to pry himself loose and succeeded briefly, but before he could begin to rise Florence had pounced once more upon him and, wrapping her arms and legs around him, held on for life, riding out his furious lunges and resistance. Florence held, squeezed and embraced as though she were subduing a wild boar. She felt a shoe slide off one foot, but now was no time to worry about that; there was an urgency to deal with.

To her surprise, she found she was managing to restrain Breed without any significant violence; he was jerking and pushing and flailing insanely, but was unable to shake her off him. It was as though Miss Dragonheel had emerged and given her the strength and stamina she needed to keep this person who was much larger and stronger than herself at bay and under control; she could handle this human storm. Also to utter surprise, she found herself having to suppress a bit of lust forming from all the physical contact with him as he twisted, squirmed against her body and limbs. *Foolish woman you---this man's snapping and erupting like Mount St. Helens and you're lusting after him don't you know his life and yours are at stake!* But she had to admit that, with a bit of effort, he'd be quite the catch.

"Let me go, let me go!" he cried. "I don't want of need your help or anyone's---"

"Frankly, kid," she quipped, "you need some loving!"

"Bianca was right," he moaned in frustration. "I am a pathetic fool. Let me fulfill everyone's---"

"*Shush!* You've fancied me as your heroine Miss Dragonheel all this time and now I'm fulfilling the part." She clasped his chin and forced him to look at her.

"It's no use---" Breed said, trying to resist.

"Breed, if you keep fighting me instead of listening I'm not going to let you up." She turned his head to face her. "You're *not* a fool," she said in a softer, reassuring tone. "And you're sure as hell not worthless or pathetic. Listen, no fool could have fascinated me with as you have both as person and artist---"

"But my art's...gone..."

"Not completely---not at all!" she said. "I went by the house and managed to gather some if it---it's in my glove compartment now. I'll be honest, Breed---a lot of it is roughed up, and I couldn't save it all, but you may still be able to salvage it. And let me say this, Hamilton: Even if *all* of it had been lost, your art's still not destroyed."

Breed's face turned incredulous through its pain. "You...saved my work...? But..."

"Is that not what a heroine's for?" she smiled wickedly, noting that he had calmed quite remarkably. "Well, since you're back to your senses, I think I can release you." She began to ready herself to rise, but he grasped her arm.

"Please," he said, almost in a whisper. "Stay, just a little longer...I..." Unable to say any more, he pulled her towards him and held her tightly, tears streaming down his cheeks.

"Very well," she complied. "But you're lucky you didn't cast me as a nun."

For a long while they held each other close, without words.

"Could this be mother love?" Florence asked herself about what she was feeling. "Or is it a slightly more risqué version of such?"

Twenty-Seven

After what seemed to be an eternity Florence opened her eyes and glanced behind her at a clock on the wall. "Oh my, she said to herself, "we have been knotted up in each other awhile have we!"

Turning back to Breed, she nudged him gently. "Hey...hey Breed," she said a little playfully, "I think a few hours of huggability's convincing enough...it's time for bed." But Breed gave no response.

"Breed---?" She nudged him a little harder.

Then a snore broke into her train of thought.

"*Breed!*" she snapped in utter disbelief as she rose to her knees over his sleeping form. "Well, *I'll be---!!! Went and FELL ASLEEP on me---*or rather *UNDER* me." She did not know whether to be delighted, outraged, humiliated or *what* at this development. *If that Dashiki Drab or some cop ever got wind of this they'd swear I either humped* *him or raped him to sleep.* Yet she wasn't all that sure that she'd have minded either---especially not the former. And she certainly was not ashamed of having held him closely all that time, partly because after all the effort she had made in subduing this big powerful John Henry of a man who was nearly young enough to be her son to boot, she had barely had a chance to rest, though she had never fallen asleep as Breed had. (Besides, he really *had* needed some loving!) *Funny---I never considered myself the maternal type, though maybe he did need a maternal body to sleep in the arms of. I wonder...was this the first time he had EVER had a maternal body (however unsuited for the task as I was) to sleep in the arms and on the breast of?*

Whatever the answer to that was, another fact was clear: Breed needed hauling into a decent bed. And only one person could do that. "Using more of her effort," Florence said to herself, "Florence Orville becomes Miss Dragonheel---again." Somehow it never occurred to her to simply wake him up, which she would realize later. But one last thing--- "Goodbye, other shoe," she sighed as she kicked off her remaining shoe. *Irony of ironies---a Dragonheel without heels.*

Step by step, stockinged foot by stockinged foot, grasping Breed's arm and torso, she hauled him up the stairway, leaning against the wall for support. It was quite a task, even with that superheroine strength of hers (heck, one could only summon power like that so much at a time), but somehow, she succeeded. It was a little easier to drag him to a guest room, fortunately she had had the door open. The easiest part of all was undressing him and pulling the covers of the bed over him. Then she sank to a chair beside the bed and watched over him. As she sat wearily in the chair, it was dawning on her that this must have been what both Dion Hapless and the Mother meant when they said she would be needed. It felt so good to be needed, to be warm and compassionate---even to be a mother figure. But it could be so taxing--- nobody had told her it would be so hard.

Twenty-Eight

For much of that night she sat in the branches of the oak, looking over and on the house, particularly at the window where Breed still slept. To her surprise she was quite up and about herself after the brief nap she had taken while she guarded him, and was quite desiring of some sort of communication as to what had occurred the night before. And she soon got that communication.

Congratulations are in store for you.

For me?   Don't tell me---you're awfully generous tonight.

Don't underestimate your success tonight so! Rather, rejoice over your passage.

Hey, I only stopped Breed from wrecking himself---not to mention my living room.

And from more than such mundane things as that.   It might even be called Breed Hamilton's moment of truth.   Had you misstepped---

I'd never have seen Breed again, eh?

That's about the size of it. You are one with the potential for great creation or great destruction, and you've certainly displayed a bit of the latter in your time.

Dion Hapless.

One such casualty.

All right, so what's next?

That's up to you now. You've tapped your energy; now's the transformative test is about to commence.

Wonderful.

Doubt all you will but now that you've become aware, it is yours.

But it was so much fun then.

*You don't believe that anymore than I do. Anyway, wasn't it a bit of---*arousing *when you---as you put it---humped Breed to sleep---*

Watch it!

You are human---not dead.

Just my luck.

Admit it.

So touché---satisfied!

You know you *are.*

I know I'm an old biddy.

So you're a late bloomer. But you're an awake bloomer now. There's hope for you.

Just---my---luck.

Twenty-Nine

By the end of a week since Breed came into her home Florence was getting more than a little concerned about him. He was really good company and helped her in various tasks around him, but there was a melancholy air about him, particularly when he looked over the remains of the art ("---and especially," she observed to herself, "the ones with the pictures of Bianca.") that she had salvaged for him.

She watched him sit forlornly, his head bent down to observe the remains of this art on a coffee table. Though he never discussed it with her, she knew what it was about. Though he had annoyed her in some ways when she had first met him and learned of his idolization of her---she'd not much thought herself capable of being idolized, and especially not after her having been found out---at least then there had been a spark, a life, an exploration, a *joie de vivre*---about him. Now that seemed to have vanished, leaving only a lost soul, and it frightened Florence, who had seen many people in this stage end up none too pleasantly, in some cases even to the grave. It frightened her even more because she knew that the methods she might have used in her days as the top agent at the Blanchstone Agency would not work here; indeed, they had contributed to some of those casualties. And the woman who relied on them was gone anyway---she could never again be that proto-Miss Dragonheel again.

I won't toughlove I won't I won't I WON'T! That was adamant in her mind. But what could she do? That approach, so easy to turn to, so ingrained into her it was---and look where it got her---a fall from quasi-grace and cold non-acknowledgement from former clients. And she wanted acknowledgement so bad---it suddenly dawned on her that her current feelings were quite similar to those of her childhood when she had been interrogated and indoctrinated into believing that she was of no importance whatsoever. How she had managed to fight and overcome all those demons---

Something came to her. *Of course!* She knew what needed to be done now. Taking a final glance at him, she made a silent move for the back door.

When she reached the front of her house on the way to the Civic, she noted something else for the first time. There was nobody there. "Huh…no Dashiki Drab," she observed to herself: Must've found some other hapless soul to harangue." Then she entered her car, started the engine, and drove off with the caution of one who did not really wish too many people to know that she was leaving.

Thirty

Virtually as if he had not noticed Florence had so much as been gone, Breed maintained his view of the tattered shreds of his art, though some interlocking (of sorts) pieces had been taped, the work looked like a series of jigsaw puzzles with most of the pieces lost forever. He could not even muster up the energy to sigh in resignation over what might have been---for his art and for Bianca.

And something dropped *POP!* onto the piles with no warning.

It was a large tablet of thick paper, followed almost instantaneously by several packs of pens and markers. Startled, he made a reflexive look up at the person who had dropped them onto his world, and who was looking down on him with warm intensity.

"Woke you up, did I?" Florence's voice was gentle, even playful---but there was an unmistakable insistence in it.

"What…is this about?" he said incredulously. "I mean, this is kind of you, but---"

"Not kind, just acknowledging the great Breed Hamilton, artist extraordinaire."

"Some artist I turned out to be...all my work...ruined..."

"Hey, why'd you think I got you this stuff? Think you're the only one who's lost his life's work? Any case, I want you to do a drawing."

His face fell. "A...drawing...? I---I don't know if I can..."

"*Wrong*, kiddo," she replied kindly yet firmly. "Listen, you owe me quite a bit, and I'm wanting some payment from you right about now." *Remember Florence, no tough talk.* "And you *know*, dear, that I've lost quite a bit of my life myself, so no excuses from you. Your first payment's due---" She kicked the table underneath the paper pad. "---right here."

"I...don't even know what you want me to do."

"Do what you want, or what you can. It just has to be done."

"Everything's so...so blocked in me..." he murmured. "All I can think of...I can think of...are those cops...laughing as they destroyed my work...and the hatred they had for...me."

"Then do *that*, Breed---get it all out of your very soul. Don't carry it inside you; it can kill you---and those cops would *love* that."

"But it's so hard," he said sadly.

"I know it is," she replied sympathetically but remained steadfast. "But you need to put something on paper, to get your process jumpstarted again---and you should know by now that I'll keep on you until you do."

"Suppose I fail---?"

"You've only failed miserably if you don't start. And you'd best start real soon, kid---" She began an embryonic chuckle. "---I've not got all day." She moved beside him and clutched his hand (*Not too hard you can gut or gore the poor guy with your dragon nails.*) "I'll be here to cheer you on if you wish."

"All right...just...don't cheer out loud...just be here."

"I won't say a word until you wish me to."

Breed heaved forward, as though making a silent yawn. He stared at the challenge awaiting him on the table. Then he proceeded to meet that challenge.

Thirty-One

Breed appeared to Florence to be like one possessed as he proceeded in doing his first post-ordeal picture. She could not quite tell what it would consist of for a long time---it was clearly not a head (or even full-person) shot of anyone; in any case, she could tell that he was working with an intensity that for all she knew he was displaying for perhaps the first time ever. "That would be quite a feather in a cap of history for me" she smiled to herself (but was not about to state aloud). She could not help but imagine a symphony in staccato rhythm in tune with Breed's effort---a staccato rhythm threatening to burst into an abrupt crescendo. She noted something was taking shape---intermingling streaks of violent red and navy blue, with interspersing of other colors. The intensity made Florence wonder if she had become Dr. Frankenstein to Breed's monster.

After a time Breed completed the picture to his apparent satisfaction and set it aside, then without another word he began work on his next project. He remained as intense as ever, though, so Florence stayed silent. "But I didn't promise, did I," she thought to herself, "to not take a peek at the thing."

She moved to a position where she could view the finished picture; the blue lines were predominant with red seemingly flowing from them. She realized to her surprise that the blue lines represented police officers, lying sprawled on the "pavement." There were two of them, and the red about them was their intermingling blood. She noted that beside each of them were a sketchily drawn badge, one saying T. HARNELL and the other saying P. HERRERA. "No doubt these were the names of those dopey officers who did this to Breed," Florence observed silently.

Breed drew in rapid yet precise succession for quite some time until he had gone through half of the notepad. By the time he had finished, he had completed three portraits, one of Bianca, one of Florence and (the last completed one) of himself, in addition to another violent depiction of police officers, two pieces consisting of painted words (almost as if in a poem), and several whose meaning Florence could not determine offhand.

She turned to look at him. He looked exhausted, as though he had run an athletic marathon instead of completing a number of drawings. She moved over behind him and placed her hands upon his shoulders, gently caressing and massaging them.

"This payment enough for you?" he inquired with a touch of sarcasm.

"*Wel-l-l-l...*" she joshed. "I really only wanted one. But I'm not about to complain."

"And you never once broke my train of thought," he said as though it were a shocking surprise.

She kicked the side of his calf in mock-indignation. "*Hey!* I gave you my word!" she snapped.

Breed merely gave a silent grin, having figuratively woken her up.

Thirty-Two

There was yet one more thing that she, Florence, could do for Breed, she realized a little later. And she did not hesitate to do just that---at least after he had stepped out for some fresh air.

Bounding to where her cell phone was, she picked it up and dialed. "Funston said Winthrop's been wanting some business for the gallery," she said to herself. "I can kill all kinds of stones with this bird."

Standing above her bed as she listened to the other end's ringing, she picked up a picture of Breed's that she had taken with her; one that she believed could best bring out the type of crowd that would patronize a place like Winthrop's.

"Studio d'Winthrop."

"Hey, Winthrop. This is Florence Orville, long time no hear."

"Long *long* time."

"Uh, yeah," she conceded. "Still can use a good exhibit?"

"Yes, but what can *you* do now---"

"Don't ask me how I did it, but there's this artist who can be pretty big pretty soon and you'll go down in history as the exhibitor who introduced him to the world."

"*Really?* What publicity that would bring! His name, what is his name, tell me!"

"Breed Hamilton."

"Ah, already a memorable name as I hear it! Show me, show me just one, Mademoiselle Florence Orville, and I'll see to it that he gets the finest grand opening. Come over, come over right now!"

"All right, all right!" she smiled. "I'll be over at once." She quickly put on a coat, and as she passed through her living room, decided to take one more of Breed's pictures ("---just to play safe," she cautioned to herself) and, stepped outside.

Hey---lucky day. Still no Dashiki Drab.

At the Studio d'Winthrop about twenty minutes later, the proprietor examined the picture Florence had shown him and was nodding with enthusiasm.

"It does appear that I've horribly misjudged you, Mademoiselle," he said. "I should not have fully believed all that bad press about you after that terrible ordeal of yours. Blemish or no blemish, you've still got that Midas touch. If only you could have brought this Breed Hamilton with you so I could meet this ingenious creator myself."

"Hey, you didn't even give me a chance to wait for him to return!" Florence quipped. "Now you'll have to wait 'till the reception. But I'll make sure he's here then."

"I shall hold you to that," Winthrop said. "I shall contact the press immediately, and send you a note with the date on it. And I shall personally see to it that you get a full mention---the weight of a petty scandal should not silence you forever. And by all means, return to this Hamilton fellow and inform him of all this. I did not mean to hold you so long."

"No problem. I'll let him know. And thank you, Winthrop."

"No, Mademoiselle, *thank you.*"

"*All right!*" she said triumphantly on her way back to the Civic. "Hamilton, you're on your way up. And *you*, Orville, are on your way *back.*" Reaching her car, she rushed in and started the engine to make the triumphant return home.

But somehow this no longer feels as smooth as process as before.

Thirty-Three

"---and he totally liked my work?" a delighted and incredulous Breed said upon receipt of the acceptance of his work.

"He did indeed," Florence smiled. "I was only able to send him two of your works but he liked them both---said you would be quite a future find."

"That's...great," he remarked, still a bit doubtful.

"Didn't think you'd get into the big time so soon, did you!"

"No...I didn't." He hung down and scratched his head, as if trying to make sense of all this.

"Not only that, but he's got a place with access to the best-known critics and art circles and cliques. You'll be the next Picasso, kiddo!" she giggled.

"I doubt that," he said amusingly. "I'd rather be the first Breed Hamilton."

"Hey, you'll be that and more," Florence said. "The Studio d'Winthrop is a class act."

"You worked with the proprietor?"

"Practically helped get him that studio when I was at Blanchstone. But as I said, I was only able to select two pieces for him to look at---sorry 'bout being so random about that without checking with you, but---"

"That's all right."

"In any case, Breed," she joshed, "stick with me and you might have your own studio someday!"

Before Breed could reply to that, Florence's telephone rang violently.

"Oh pshaw," she groaned as if it had ruined her goodwill towards Breed. "Let me deal with this." She rushed to answer it.

For some reason the violent ring suggested to Breed that something was very urgent. Turning to Florence, he realized, though he could not make out what was being said on the other end, her body language revealed that it was definitely not good news.

"Yes---yes---" she said brokenly, "I'm on my way." She hung up the phone and moved upstairs, returning moments later, hurriedly putting on a coat.

"Is...something wrong...?" he inquired with trepidation.

"I'm afraid so," she near-whispered. "Not with the exhibit, mind you; but---but---" Somehow she could not get the exact words to form in her voice. "Someone needs me at the hospital---I'll explain later when I get back." She bolted out the door almost as soon as she had finished.

Breed watched her quickly enter her car and explode off into the distance through the front window. "Has to be of critical importance," he thought to himself.

With nothing better to do at the moment, he turned to the box containing the two works Florence had taken to show to the Studio d'Winthrop. Curious as to which ones they had been (he had been so busy making new works in his creative burst that he had occasionally lost track of those he had done previously), he opened it and pulled out the contents to see.

Upon viewing them he found himself surprisingly nonplussed---and perhaps a little disappointed.

Thirty-Four

It struck Florence as bizarrely peculiar that she was rushing at breakneck speed to a hospital on behalf of someone she didn't even like in the first place---or seemed to like her either for that matter. "But stranger things have happened to me," she thought to herself. *Do tell.*

She had managed to pull a few details about the circumstances from the doctor who had called her. Two policemen had shot Dashiki Drab (*riddled* him! she would have put mildly) about a week and a half ago on a street corner about a half-mile from her place ("At least that explains why he's not been around to harass me," she mused). It would not have surprised her if he had somehow carried on with the cops, or someone who in frustration had alerted them, in such a way as to provoke them into shooting him, but it would have no more surprised her if they'd done so simply because they felt like it or because they could. "Mistaken identity---*ha!*" she snapped. "*Alleged* vagrancy---*she-e-e-it!*" That was one more the cops owed her, and she hadn't forgotten what they had done to Breed either, or for that matter, their meeting with her on the hill.

"Yep, one more thing they owe," she thought to herself, "forcing me to drive all the way to see to a dying man who doesn't even like me!" Yet she felt compelled to drive on, to see this small mission through. If that fool rebuffs her---well, he's done *that* before. Nothing would stop *her* from trying to do right.

She had finally reached the hospital; at the first entrance to the parking lot she pulled onto the premises.

Making her way to the hospital emergency room, she motioned the receptionist.

"Uh, excuse me, I'm here in a response to a call from Dr. Turner---"

"Your name, please?"

"Florence Orville."

"Very well, I have his note." Turned to the intercom. "Dr. Turner, your visitor is here---Dr. Reed Turner, there's a Miss Florence Orville to see you."

Florence sank into a nearby couch while she waited for Dr. Turner to arrive. "How bizarre," she thought to herself. "How peculiar...that I'm here to see to the last wish of a dying man who never liked me…and how funny authority shifts from intoxicant to battery acid when the tables turn."

She jerked upon realizing she had absolutely no idea how that latter thought occurred to her. "Easy, Florence…everything's been jumping at you since…oh this awareness is quite a pest, you know."

"Ms. Orville?"

She looked up. It was a stocky, distinguished coal-black doctor.

"I'm Dr. Turner. My apologies for any inconvenience."

"It was surprising," she said, "but I suppose necessary."

She rose to her feet and they began to move into a corridor, where Dr. Turner pressed an up button for an elevator.

"How is---" she began, then suddenly remembered she did not even have a name for Dashiki Drab, "---how…is he?"

"Worse than we initially thought," Dr. Turner said gravely. "He might not even survive the night. If someone on staff hadn't recognized your name when he mentioned it and made a wild guess by checking your number---he might have died all alone---whoops, there's the elevator. Let's go."

"There's something I don't understand, Ms. Orville," Dr. Turner said during the elevator ride. "When our personnel inspected the meager belongings he had, they came upon this."

He handed the card to Florence, who looked carefully at it. It was a state identification card, but what alarmed her was the area where the holder's name and address were, or would have been, for it was scratched and scribbled so severely that one could not make it out at all. It was as if Dashiki Drab had not wanted anyone to learn his real name.

"That's odd indeed," she replied. "Wonder why Das---*he* would be so hell-bent on concealing his identity?"

"And it looks like we'll never know," Dr. Turner said. "You were the only one of those few associates we could learn he had that we were able to contact. A most bizarre case if you ask me---" The elevator doors opened. "Oh, here we are."

"I'll do what I can, Dr. Turner," Florence said as they stepped out of the elevator into the hospital corridor. "But I must warn you that I don't really know very much about him either. He just...forced his way into my life, and he never said anything about his background to me."

"I'm not surprised," Dr. Turner replied. "From what police reports say, he did that quite often with people. Okay, this is the room." He opened the door and held it to let Florence in before entering himself.

As Florence gestured to return the card to Dr. Turner, her eyes caught something. The birth date. Though the month and day were near unrecognizable, the year was barely readable---and she gasped silently upon noticing it was the same as her own. Though Dashiki Drab appeared years older than she, they were actually about the same age!

"Oh...my...goodness...!" she gasped to herself, realizing the full gravity of that knowledge.

Thirty-Five

Upon looking at the emaciated, frail figure of Dashiki Drab, slumped in a hospital bed with various bandages wrapped about his form and various tubings attached to him and flanked by two nurses, Florence felt something within her break deeply. They were not exaggerating about his condition; he looked as though he really could die at any moment. She had long wanted to be free of him, but not like this.

Making sure of each step as though she were walking on extremely fragile ice, she made her way to the bed. "Oh---! He's even more gaunt than when we last met," she observed to herself.

"Well it finally took your bourgeois butt long enough woman!"

"That's Dashiki Drab all right!" Florence snapped to herself. The edge was definitely there, though its volume was now that of a parched croak. But she stood her ground. Dying or not, he wasn't driving her off this time!

Yet his next words surprised her, as did their tone. "What the hell'm I doing with you? You...you ain't the one I've been riding no more. You changin' Florence Orville. You changing on me, probably mostly changed by now. Got no business bothering you no more...not that I'll be able to anyway."

"I---guess I'm glad to hear that from you," she replied, trying to be as cordial as possible. "But what makes you think I've changed?"

"Still the headstrong one ain'tcha!" he grinned painfully. "You'll find out…smart lady like you always do. Just my luck I'll not see the full results on you---motherfucking pigs."

"At least tell the doctor and nurses who you are."

"Across the oceans and to a far land…that's the riddle of all time, which it is for me to fly to who I am, and get back to what was lost at last!"

This was said so smugly that Florence became quite furious. *"This here's no time for riddles!"* she snapped. "Can't you see---" She stopped all of a sudden, realizing her indignation had no place to go, for he whom she had dubbed Dashiki Drab was---

"Gone," Dr. Turner sighed. "What a sad way to go."

"If only we'd been able to learn his name at least," said the younger of the nurses.

"What a terrible waste," the elder one sighed.

"It was a waste," Florence said musingly, "but not necessarily of his own making. And his name…his name was lost centuries before he was born, stolen from the motherland just as the ancestors had been, and all remaining connections were shouted, beaten, wrenched away upon settlement in a land far in distance and foreign in virtually every way from that which the ancestors had known. The name he would have had was forever lost, but now he has begun his flight to the motherland---to his true identity and name."

She had been walking slowly towards the door as she spoke, but stopped upon reaching it. She turned to face Dr. Turner and the nurses.

"That was the meaning of his riddle," she continued. "His true name was lost. No other name, be it his birth name, or any other, or my own name for him, Dashiki Drab---mattered."

"Nor will the one we'll have to list him under," Dr. Turner replied in a way that indicated he understood all this. "John Doe."

"Indeed," Florence nodded, and turned and left the room.

(Later she would question herself as to how she had come up with that answer so instantaneously.)

Thirty-Six

Up up up she pulled and pushed herself, fantasizing herself as a sleek panther (albeit a--- *maturing* ---one) making her way to a perch from which she could observe and perform some sort of act for a fallen warrior, almost as one would do for a most honorable enemy.

"Am I getting a bit long up there for this," she wondered to herself, taking note of her own breathing form against the cool, sturdy bark of the trunk and branches. "Maybe...or maybe not. It's all their fault for my being up there in a sense their bitching and moaning about how un-*lay-dee*-like it was to do this thing. Now I'm one walking case of arrested development---just as Dashiki Drab was--- one walking case of accelerated development.

"You talk too much Florence," she continued, both in word and ascension. "That's all over now and nobody can tell you what to do not to do or how to do. Keep moving on up woman to your true self Miss Dragonheel!" And she did just that. ("But could that mean that Dashiki Drab has moved on *down?*" she could not help inquiring.)

She finally reached the summit of her intention this night---a point in the middle of the tree where two of the branches made a fork (a "non-pineapple upside down fork," she dubbed it with amusement) and where she could brace herself, hands and feet, on the branches and look down at the ground below.

And then she let the tears flow.

They flowed, dropping from her eyes and face, dripping down to whatever lay below. She fantasized that her eyes were the open floodgates releasing the stream of tears to flow down her face, then waterfall to the grounds below to form a small lake of water in which (somehow) life could rejuvenate once again. Of course, this was all symbolic as far as the fallen warrior Dashiki Drab was concerned.

In her scenario, the sea her tears was creating was that onto which a boat could be sailed, and into the middle of which Dashiki Drab's ashes could be scattered as the now-freed spirit, restored to its true age, could fly back to the motherland and to its own identity. She could not claim the body or contact any survivors (assuming that there had been any), but could use her still-vast knowledge of laws and stuff to maneuver things so he could at least find a bit of the security he had apparently never found while alive. (Which is what she had had done. However repugnant she had believed he was, nobody deserved his fate.)

At last there were no more tears to shed, and the sea shrank down to the grass terrain of the back yard hosting the tree into which she was wrapped around, observant of all.

"Have a safe trip home, Dashiki Drab," she said wearily.

She remained in her perch for a long period before finally descending.

Thirty-Seven

People were slowly accumulating into Studio d'Winthrop, Florence observed, most dressed to the eighteens and displaying the awes and oohs of patrons eagerly awaiting the new find of the century ("which seemed to happen quite often per year, much less decade or century," she noted with not a little disdain).

She wondered what her hostility to all that was about. It used to tickle her so. And she sensed it wasn't really because of the recent loss of her adversary Dashiki Drab. "Well, whatever it is," she mused to herself, "I'll have to watch you, Florence, to make sure you don't make a Miss Dragonheel out of yourself here."

She passed by the room where Breed stood, looking much the worse in a rented tuxedo in which he looked forlorn, obviously neither accustomed to or even interested in looking so formal.

"Hey, chin up!" she joshed. "It's your opening day, Breed Hamilton---the first day of a brand new life for you!"

"Some life," he replied with not a little embarrassment. "Now, Florence, this is awfully sweet of you to arrange all this, but---"

"*Sweet?*" She barked with laughter. "Well, maybe a little...but remember, Breed, that this *is* a capitalistic society. So relax…everything's about to begin. See ya." And she quickly departed.

But when she was out of the room, she involuntarily remarked, "…*this is a capitalistic society?*…Somehow that didn't feel too good to say…rather something very wrong."

"It's about to begin," beamed Winthrop to Florence a short time later. "Look at this crowd---I can't believe this---and you created it all!"

"Breed did most of the creating," Florence replied, "but other than that, this should convince you and everyone else that Florence Orville hasn't lost her touch."

"*I* never believed you had---honest!" Winthrop said as if he had been accused of forgetting. "But enough of this---I must do the introduction!"

"Don't break anything," she called as he moved to the podium. She turned to see if Breed had arrived. Realizing that he had not, she attempted to move to look for him, but the crowd around her had become too thick for her to penetrate.

"Oh *wonderful,*" she groaned. "Breed's about to miss out on his own debut! Just…our…luck. And Winthrop's about to speak."

"Ladies and gentlemen," Winthrop called out, "your attention, please."

As the crowd quieted down to some degree (though never completely), he elected to continue. "Tonight we are gathered here to witness and welcome the arrival of a great and stunning young talent on the scene…a talent whose very name inspires the world to come up with more such as himself, a talent most aptly named...*Breed Hamilton!*"

"Breed...*where are you...!*" Florence thought frantically. "Damn this sardine crowd---how giddy they're acting!"

"But...since our Mister Hamilton is obviously a most modest gentleman, we shall respect his desire for anonymous identity while he lets his work speak for itself and allow his work to do just that. So-o-o-o, as they say---" He grasped a corner of the covering. "*Voila!*"

He pulled the covering away, and in that instant the hubbub and exuberance of the crowd vanished, as though shot away by a light switch. Florence turned, wondering what had happened, and gasped with horror, for there was Breed's portrait of the bloodied police officers with the T. HARNELL and P.HERRERA badges with the violent sketches all around. Under the picture was a caption "THE BEST FANTASY OF THE WOULD-BE "BOYS."

"That...*that---!*" Florence said, her tone becoming angrier as she realized what Breed had done. "I swear I'll---! *OOO-H-H-H!!*"

She forced herself to stop right there and, squeezing her way through the astonished crowd, and breathing genuine Miss Dragonheel fire, she marched toward the room in which she had last seen him.

"What the---?" "What kind of trick is that Winthrop pulling?" "Oh my oh my...the shame..." "*Who the hell does that Winthrop think he is!*" "*THAT FLORENCE ORVILLE WILL NEVER WORK IN THIS MILIEU AGAIN!!!*"

The cries of shock, disorientation and outrage serenaded Breed as a favorite song might have. A devious smile was on his face as he savored his triumph. *Hated to do that to Florence, I know, she meant very well for me but I just couldn't let those portraits she selected serve as my definitive work; besides, I'm just not meant for this kind of rat race.* Moreover, he thought he had recognized the two officers who had roughed him up there, and, though he could not have known that they'd be there when he had switched the portraits, he felt pleased to have found a opportunity to get back at them if only symbolically. His only regret as he moved in rhythm to the pandemonium about him was that it would severely hurt Florence's chances of ever again winning her high-powered influence back. But something told him that that was not nearly as big a loss as it might first appear.

But try telling that, he realized upon looking at the doorway, to the woman standing there with murderous fury in her eyes.

Thirty-Eight

"I really ought to *kill* you!" Florence snarled with a quiet restraint that was barely holding back an explosion. "Or kick your miserable ass this instant. Perhaps both will be sufficient."

"And no doubt you can do either," he replied casually. "A very powerful woman you are, both as Florence Orville and as Miss Dragonheel. Your power is such that it's most frightening. I wouldn't stand a chance."

"You know what you've done," she said, almost as a threat, "to yourself and to me both."

"Guilty as charged," he admitted. "But those portraits you selected were made in one of my weaker moments. Even if it had fooled those characters for long, the true me would have become clear to them sooner or later."

"And by then you would've had a foothold!" she retorted. "Did it ever occur to you----do you even realize what you've done---"

"To my prospects...or *yours?*" he inquired.

"*Of course to mine!*" she remarked indignantly. "You realize what effort I had to make so I---" She stopped suddenly, realizing something in Breed's words. "*I---*"

He did not seem to notice her hesitation; instead he hung his head down in apparent resignation. "Well, Florence, it's really been nice being with you, and God knows I owe you an infinite amount. I'll...I'll be packing up and be out of your life for good by morning."

She shot her head around to face him.

"*Don't...you...dare,*" she hissed. "You don't get rid of Miss Dragonheel *that* easy!"

"Excuse me---but might you be...Mr. Hamilton?"

This sudden interjection caused Florence and Breed to turn to the doorway, where a smallish woman about Florence's age and seemingly of Native American descent stood.

"Yes, Madam, that's me," Breed replied.

"Thank goodness you really were here," the woman said. "I must say, that really was a fast one you and Ms. Orville pulled on the clientele. I sometimes get invited to these things, for I, too, am the proprietor of a gallery, and for better and worse,

117

of one the mayor has publicized quite a bit. I admit, you two have provided the biggest laugh for me yet, and I know how bizarre these things---and these *people*---can get." She handed both of them a card. "Since it looks like your work won't be long for this gallery, Mr. Hamilton, might I suggest to you and your agent Ms. Orville that you exhibit at my gallery instead? It's not quite as...*haute couture*...as here, but I suspect it's better suited to your work of subversion."

Florence's face widened upon looking at the card, for she had instinctively overlooked that option. "Of course you fool Florence!" she reproached herself. "Your old Blanchstone Agency mentality did you in again! Of course of course! Like it did when you selected the wrong pictures for Breed!"

She ceased just in time to hear Breed say "yes" to the offer.

"And I'm sure, Ms. Orville," the woman said, "that with an agent like you watching out for him, Mr. Hamilton will go far. Call me tomorrow and we can make arrangements." Then she exited before Florence could respond.

"But I'm not...officially...his agent," she could only say to the air.

Breed turned triumphantly to face her. "And you thought we were all through!"

"Don't push it, kid," she warned half-jokingly. "My foot's still hungry for your derriere."

Thirty-Nine

Hahahahahahahahahahahaha---
Stop laughing already!
Haha did the student turn teacher on you!
All right I'm big enough to know when I've been wrong. Now quit rubbing it in. It did take quite some doing to get that work of his out of Studio d'Winthrop in one piece after all that commotion and everything.

And you won despite yourself you're an agent again, and mustn't discount all those letters of support either. Didn't expect that did you!
So it wasn't such a disaster for me or Breed after all. But I'll never again be sought after by any big agency or corporation or anyone I once worked with.

As if they'd been working on your behalf all along---really tragic! Admit it---was it not just wonderful to stick it to them for a change? Come on, out with it!
Okay, okay! It *was! After* the fact.

And besides, you found you do have quite a number of fans and folks in your corner should you get to be too lonely a subversive.
Touché.

But I must admit I really was surprised when you wouldn't let Breed leave your premises. You really were ready to slaughter him.
Because, nosy, I realized that us folks *have* tended to offer food and shelter to share what we can with each other. That's one tradition I find I rather like. Another surprise for little old me.

Anything to do with the loss of Dashiki Drab?

Partly, I think. Maybe if I'd done for him what I eventually came to do for Breed, he might still be alive. But alas, we'll never know for sure.

Well, it's definitely not too late for Breed. You should hear some of the buzz about the exhibit in its true location.

I have heard it.

So the old dog can learn her some new tricks.

The old *dragon*, clown. Dragon*heel* to you. Now buzz off before the next new trick I learn becomes how to ditch *you.*

Wouldn't miss that. You almost don't need me anymore you're healing up so fast.

Don't you be too quick to pack up and go. Maybe I'll heal---or is it *heel*---

Groan---!

---no further; maybe I've found a cure in a portion of my so-called illness---my "craziness."

Oh...my...goodness...!

Quiet now, here comes Breed.

Breed walked out into the yard below where Florence sat perched, not too far above him, in the oak, like the curious panther. He was holding in his hands a just completed portrait of Bianca, the head, neck and shoulders of which were quite well-defined, but the definition below became fainter until there was no outline for what should have been her lower legs, ankles and feet---

("...a sort of *disappearance*," Florence observed. "God...how forlorn he looks. Still feeling for poor Bianca, and you, foolish Florence, nearly forgot about that you were so caught up in your own loss of Dashiki Drab and Breed's sabotaging your petty attempt to return to the rat race. Well, amazing Miss Dragonheel, you almighty protector, do what Breed would imagine you doing back in the day---spring into action!")

Breed set the portrait on the ground and stood above it, looking silently at it. "For you, Dona Bianca," he whispered shakily, "wherever you are."

The next moment he jumped with a start when something pointed and smooth jabbed him right below the shoulder blade. Not a finger, and definitely not a knife, but it *had* been deliberate, even a thrust. Whirling about on reflex, he realized he had come closer to the oak than he had expected he was, and that Florence was seated in it above him giggling. It was the toe of her stiletto that had poked him.

"Wake up!" she beamed. "And c'mon up here to keep me company."

He shook his head. "*What* have I got myself into?" he thought to himself with a mixture of amusement and annoyance as he ascended the tree, with ready assistance from her. Still new to him, but he was getting the hang of it. "It will always amaze me how she can function in a tree attired as she is and at her age. Perhaps she really is some sort of heroine after all."

"Have a name for your latest one there?" she inquired.

"Tentatively---*Bianca the Disappeared.*"

He closed his eyes and hung his head. Florence grasped and pulled him close to her, allowing him to grieve and allowing herself to absorb the grief, hoping she could prevent it from overcoming him completely in this way. She grieved herself as well, but knew she could handle her own overflow. In a way this was worse than the loss of Dashiki Drab, for at least his fate was known and could allow for some sort of closure. But Bianca's loss might never offer such a luxury.

Florence did not know what to say to Breed, but something told her it was best simply to be there for him. That appeared to be sound advice, for not once during these moments did Breed lose any sort of composure.

"Just needed a shoulder to cry on," she clichéd to herself, without sarcasm.

Forty

They remained seated near each other in the oak tree, looking over Florence's yard with the portrait *Bianca the Disappeared* leaning on it.

"You plan to act on those offers you've been getting these past few days?" Breed inquired of her.

She frowned in mock-annoyance. "You can be such a pain," she joked before turning a bit more serious. "But I don't know yet...now that the opportunity's there, I find I'm at a complete loss. I suppose, though, I should at least reply to them; I owe them that much."

"But you'd be the best agent, Florence."

"Try telling *that* to my old Blanchstone colleagues and clients now, kiddo! And, besides, mister---" She shot a finger at his face. "---I've got enough trouble with you. I've still not forgotten *your* little sabotage."

"I promise I won't sabotage this---honest!" he grinned.

"Still," she remarked, "it did give me a rather wicked idea---suppose I take in some of these clients-to-be…why, we could infiltrate all those staid studios and overpriced hotels and restaurants and such. Sneaky, ain't it?"

"That's quite ingenious," Breed agreed. "You know…we're making quite a pair."

"Yep," she mock-snarled, jutting her thumb in his direction. "My little Breed. Some little Margie you are."

"And you're a most beauteous Vern."

"*Wait a second!* You're not old enough to---oh, never mind!" They both burst into laughter, after which she continued, "You're right, Breed; we are becoming quite a pair…a different kind of pair---you Robin, me Batman!"

"Isn't Robin a feminine name?"

"It's gender-neutral, you---!" she retorted, bursting into laughter again and taking him with her. "See what trouble you are by yourself! Always pushing my buttons!"

"But you're Miss Dragonheel. Surely I can't dent you that bad."

"I got news for you, Breed---you're pretty mighty in your own right, definitely more so than you realize, and I think you know a few of my weaknesses by now. In any case, we'll pick our own aliases. Mine's Miss Dragonheel---what's your code-name?"

"Breed Hamilton," he grinned.

"Boy, for an artist, you're so un-original at times," she grumbled.

"Well, you knew keeping me around was dangerous when you chose to do so," he replied. "You should've just kicked me out when you had the chance."

"Not on your life!" she mock-snapped. "*I* was kicked out and look what happened to me. No way would I wish that on anyone else, least of all on purpose. Also, I'm not sure I ought to call this *my* property anymore...this's really *ours* now, and no argument from you."

"Look out world," Breed said. "Should we respond to the inquiries?"

"Of course," Florence said. "This is a Dynamic Duo come to adjust some *attitude*, and such vile scourges as the Market!"

"Free enterprise!" Breed said.

"And that diabolical elite the Private Sector!" Florence remarked. "Join with me, Breed, and let's start the planned alliance!" They clutched their hands and embraced each other.

Thus was born a partnership in the oak tree dominating the backyard of Florence Orville, a.k.a. Miss Dragonheel, and of Breed Hamilton.

Garrett Murphy lives in Oakland, CA, and has written several chapbooks of poetry and prose, among them *None Dare Call it Making Sense in An American Lesson, Call 9-1-1 (and Mister Punch), Up in the Attic as of Many Years Later, Mother Nature Has Become a Terrorist!, 8 Book, You Can't Be a Hero in Your Dreams,* and *I, Eye!* He has also had works published in the *Sacred Grounds Anthology,* the *New Now Now New Millennium Turn-On Anthology, Street Spirit,* and *At Home on the Land of the Dead,* among others. *Yang But Yin: The Legend of Miss Dragonheel* is the first of his novels and his second entirely prose work to see publication.

Email:
gsmurphy15@msn.com

Website:
www.garrettmurphywriter.org

23592526R00069

Made in the USA
Charleston, SC
27 October 2013